NOT SO GENEROUS HOSPITALITY

The one on my horse—but not my saddle, I noticed—said, "There's nothing at the ranch for the likes of you, bub." He gave me a look like I was a bug on the wall that ought to be swatted. . . . "You best turn around and go back."

"I'm hungry, mister. You wouldn't turn a man away hungry, would you?"

"Bub, we already did that. Now turn around and get the hell outta here before we teach you some manners."

"But you wouldn't—" I didn't have time to finish the rest of it. The SOB jabbed with his spurs, and my own damned horse bolted forward and slammed me hard with his nigh shoulder.

I hadn't been expecting that, them coming at me without a by-your-leave or a par'n-me, and I got knocked flat. I landed on a rock that hit hard in the small of my back, and the air went whooshing right out of me. I felt the stab of pain in that area, then the back of my head smacked down just as hard. From the inside it sounded like a melon being thumped, and I commenced to feel all numb and tingly. . . .

LEFT TO DIE

FRANK RODERUS

BERKLEY BOOKS, NEW YORK

P WES R688Le

This is a work of fiction. Names, characters, places, and incidents are either the product of the author's imagination or are used fictitiously, and any resemblance to actual persons, living or dead, business establishments, events, or locales is entirely coincidental.

LEFT TO DIE

A Berkley Book / published by arrangement with
the author

PRINTING HISTORY
Berkley edition / September 2000

The Penguin Putnam Inc. World Wide Web site address is
http://www.penguinputnam.com

ISBN: 0-425-17637-1

PRINTED IN THE UNITED STATES OF AMERICA

10 9 8 7 6 5 4 3 2 1

THE SONS OF bitches came sneaking up on me out of the night, and I have to say that they were awfully good at it. Or some of them were. I didn't hear nor suspect a thing, they were that good. But then what would you expect from snakes in the grass?

The first I knew there was anything going on, I heard the clunk of a rock moving and then a muttered curse just after. Stone must've turned under somebody's foot, I guess.

That was plenty enough to tell me I was in trouble, so I grabbed up my carbine and spun around into a low crouch to carry me away from the fire and into the trees uphill from where the sound had been.

It was too late for that. I wasn't halfway to those trees when two men stepped out of the very spot I'd been heading for. They were already there, already in position, already had me cold as a sporting woman's heart.

I say they had me and so they did, but if there is one thing I am not, it's a quitter. I had my carbine in my hand and my pistol on my belt. Neither of these boys had his weapon cocked.

I might have taken them. I still think I probably could've.

But not the rest of them. Before I had time to cut the dogs loose—thank goodness it was a split second before and not a half second after—three more came out to where I could see them.

These ones had guns in hand too, and at least one of them was carrying a two-shoot shotgun that was leveled at my belly and holding steady there. If there is one thing that will get my attention, it is a shotgun.

So now I was looking at five and there was at least that one more downhill, the one I'd heard stumble and grumble, and the prospects of shooting my way clear looked to be what you might call kind of poor.

I am stubborn, like I said. But I am not stupid.

I straightened up and smiled and said, "Howdy, fellas. Set down and I'll put a pot o' coffee on to boil."

It did not seem a very good sign to me that not a one of them smiled back or so much as let the muzzle of his gun sag down toward the ground.

✦ 2 ✦

"DROP 'EM," A tall bird with a scraggly mustache demanded.

"Be all right if I lay them down instead? We wouldn't want anything going off accidental, now would we?"

"Mister, you do whatever you please. Try and shoot if you like, we don't care. Just save us the trouble of hanging you if you do."

I laid my carbine down nice and slow and careful, then used the tips of two fingers to fetch my Colt out of the leather and did the same with it. I wasn't entirely sure it was the right thing to do, what with them talking hanging and all, but hanging later seemed a sight more attractive a prospect than being cut to pieces right now.

The tall one grunted when I was disarmed. He stepped a little nearer and gave me a close looking over for a couple moments, then demanded, "Where's the money?"

"Ah, now that makes things clearer, don't it?" I said, just as pleasant and mild as I knew how. "I was kinda confused for a minute there, you talkin' about hanging and all." I pointed to my saddlebags laying half underneath my saddle, over where I'd laid out my bed ready for the night. "My wherewithal is in there. Help yourself, boys, then if it's all the same t' you, I'd as leave bid you a pleasant good night."

This was something of a lie since I did have a little traveling money in the right-side bag there. But most of what I had on me—and it was considerable—was in a money belt worn down low inside my britches. They were sure welcome to the saddlebags, though.

One of them—turned out there were seven in all now that they'd all come into the firelight—fetched up my bags and rooted around inside. He wasn't very tidy about it, damn him. He'd pull something out, look it over, and then toss it onto the ground. Except for my favorite folding knife. It was a custom-made deal with three blades, one of them a regular blade, one a curved blade with only the inside belly sharp and the tip end blunt for gutting game without cutting the intestines and stuff inside, and the stout middle blade a really nice saw. It was intended for sawing bones but came in handy for other things too. I really liked that knife. I'd had it for years. Until now. The sonuvabitch saw what a fine knife it was and stuck it into his own back pocket.

"Go right ahead an' help yourself to whatever you want there," I said. And I suppose I should've known better, but my voice was maybe more than a little bit laced with sarcasm.

The guy gave me the evil eye and made an extremely vulgar suggestion. He also appropriated my wire cutters and a nearly brand-new, hardly-ever-had-any-snot-in-it blue bandanna.

When he came to my money pouch he tugged the drawstring open, peered inside, and tossed it to the tall guy with the mustache. Dumb SOB didn't have sense enough to close it first, so some coins spilled out. I guess I could've been helpful and picked them up for my visitors, but I stood where I was instead, thinking it was a darn good thing I'd acquired that money belt recently.

"This ain't all of it," the tall one growled. "Where's all the payroll money you stole?"

Now there, I have to say, he lost me. I honest-to-Pete

had no idea what payroll money he might've been talking about.

I frowned a little and gave him my most innocent and inoffensive look and told him exactly that.

I kinda think they didn't believe me, for the next thing I knew, I more heard than felt a hard thump on the back of my head, likely from a rifle butt or suchlike, and was out cold before I hit the ground.

EVER HAD YOUR hands tied tight behind your back? It is not comfortable. Not even a little bit. Whoever tied it must've been real scared that I might get loose and, I don't know, slap them all to death or something, because I was tied hand and foot just as tight as a hog being trussed for slaughter. Which, come to think of it, was closer to the truth than I wanted to contemplate.

I woke up lying on my side with my cheek pressed against hard, cold gravel that scoured my face when I moved and hurt like hell. The fact that the gravel was still cold on my skin told me that I hadn't been out too long.

I was cold in other ways too. There was a wind rising and the smaller limbs on the pines were starting to dance and bob. I could hear the sad, low soughing of it and feel the sharp drop in temperature. Neither one of those things contributed much to the moment.

And my hands hurt. They'd been tied long enough to start aching and tingling.

"Bastards," I said to no one in particular. I couldn't see any reason not to let them know my opinion, seeing as they were adopting such an unfriendly attitude anyway.

The reward for my honesty was a kick low in the back, somewhere in the vicinity of my kidneys. The only thing that kept it from being worse than it was was the fact that the SOB's boot grazed my wrist back there, so that absorbed some of the thump.

"Care to untie me and try that again, you cowardly piece of moldy dog shit?"

He kicked me again. I suppose I should've known he'd do that, and kept my mouth shut. But I expect I'd have said it exactly the same even if I had thought the likely responses through.

"Hold up, Dave." The voice sounded familiar. I twisted my head around and raised up just a little so I could see across the fire in the direction of the speaker. It was the tall one with the mustache again. It was plain that he was in charge. Especially so when the guy who liked to use his boots left off and went over to hunker beside the fire. Before he did that, though, he grunted something under his breath to show he didn't like not being allowed to kick a guy who was on the ground and couldn't fight back. Real nice fella, Dave. I looked him over close so as to make sure I would remember him the next time we met. Squat and swarthy little son of a bitch with a mole on his left cheek and eyebrows bushy enough to fill a mattress ticking if you mowed them short.

Naw, I wouldn't want to do that, I decided. Son of a bitch probably had lice.

The one with the mustache came over to stand in front of me. I wasn't entirely sure that was an improvement, though. If he decided to do some kicking his own self, I'd get it in the belly. Better the back than the front, I thought. And I will admit that I'd had experience enough before to know my preferences, as I have been known to unwisely engage in fisticuffs a time or two in the past and odds be damned.

"Something you want, asshole?" If I couldn't reach him, I could anyway insult him.

"Your name," he told me. "And the four hundred dollars that's missing from the payroll money." He held up the money belt, which I hadn't noticed was in his hand until just that moment. Dammit, they'd gone and found it. Probably when they were trussing me up. They must've felt it. Or maybe one of them'd had sense enough to search for hidden treasures. Point was, they'd gone and found it. That didn't please me much.

On the other hand, there are things in life that are more important than money. Breathing comes to mind as one of them.

"I don't know what you're talking about," I said.

"Sure you do. We counted an even five thousand here. You stole five thousand four hundred. And we know damn good and well you haven't been anyplace to spend it. You didn't have time for that. So what'd you do with that four hundred?"

"Look, mister, I don't know who you think I am or what you think I done, but the truth is, that five thousand dollars is money I'm carrying on my way to Santa Fe. I sold a herd of horses in California. That's where I got the five thousand. And I'm going to Santa Fe to meet a man who's willing to sell his freight outfit—wagons and contracts and everything—for that price. I figure to get out of the horse-hunting business, quit chasing after them lickety-split and tail over toenails, and start looking at their butts instead. Nice, quiet, calm, slow-moving butts pulling wagons that aren't like to throw a man or stomp on him nor otherwise bust him up.

"As for your payroll, mister, I have no idea what you are talking about or who it was stolen from. Nor who did the stealing. All I can tell you is that the thief wasn't me. And that, sir, is the honest-to-God truth of the matter. That money just is *not* your missing payroll."

"You're lying, of course. And I suppose it won't really matter all that much about the four hundred. If you don't want to tell us, that's your privilege. Don't have to tell us your right name either, although if you want to I'd be willing to notify your family for you. In a decent way. I wouldn't tell them what end you came to. I'll promise you that." He shrugged. "Give me your name and who it is you want notified. I'll write it down and tend to it soon as we get back to town," he said.

The wind gusted and groaned but I wasn't honestly sure if it was the cold on that wind that was putting a chill into my bones, or if it was the pretty much inescapable reason why a man might offer to write a letter to a man's folks that was getting to me.

They'd mentioned hanging?

Damned if I wasn't beginning to think they were serious about it.

Dead serious.

✤ 4 ✤

THE WIND GOT even worse, commencing to howl and the pines thrash around like they were in pain. The air felt wet and soon there were raindrops falling too. Not a lot of them. Just a few scattered here and there. But they were big and so cold you had to think they were the next thing to sleet. Any colder and it would start to sleet and then to snow. Which would have been an improvement over rain. Give me snow over a cold rain anytime.

Not that it was either snow or rain these boys were fixing to give me.

The cold I felt in that wind and weather wasn't anything to the chill that froze my gut when one of the seven, a thin man with lank, greasy blond hair, came over and hunkered down by my feet.

I'd had a faint inkling of hope that he was gonna cover me up or something, as I was lying there on the bare ground exposed to the cold.

Instead what the son of a bitch done was to reach down and twist my boots off. First one and then the other. He held them up to the sole of his own footwear, which I could see then was wore out, with worn-through holes in the bottoms and the leather at the sides so cracked it was split apart too.

My boots were a tad too big for him, but he didn't seem to care about that. He grunted once, pulled his boots off, and put mine on. He didn't wear socks, and his feet were filthy. It really peeved me to see my good boots on feet like his.

I couldn't help but notice that he never once looked me in the face while he was occupied with stealing my boots.

And he didn't bother trying to stick his old ones onto my feet neither. He tossed the old ones aside, stood up, and stamped his feet to settle them into my boots. He smiled when he did that, and I expect they must've felt pretty good to him.

Personally, I hoped he tripped in them and broke his damned neck when he fell.

"Dammit, Cap," one of the men complained, "it's fixing to come a blue norther, and I didn't bring no slicker with me."

"Take his," the tall leader of this miserable pack said. "He won't be needing it."

"Fine, but let's do what's got to be done here and get the hell gone. I want to get down off this mountain before the worst of it hits or heaven knows what it'll turn into."

The man called Cap—could've been either a name or a title, I supposed—grunted something that I couldn't hear.

The squat little bastard with the pointed boot toes and a yen to use them sure heard him, though, for he got up and fetched out a coil of rope—my own, stole off my own saddle I saw—and busied himself with tossing the business end over a close by tree limb.

Jesus God!

Two of them—not Cap, who seemed to think he was above such manual labor or something—came over and took me underneath the armpits. They lifted me up and dragged me over toward the tree.

"You can't do this. I haven't had a trial. I didn't even do what you think I did. I never stole that payroll. You're making a mist—"

The guy on my right side thumped me in the head with his fist—I hope he broke his damned hand—and Dave, who had hold of the rope, planted a hard right hand into my upper belly. That took the wind out of me and made me be quiet although only because I didn't have breath enough to speak.

I would've bent over if I could but they had me held upright and stood me there, gulping for air, while that SOB Dave draped my own catch rope over my head and pulled the loop tight. It wasn't a thirteen-turn hangman's noose, of course, just a plain old working rope with a leather hondo at the business end, but Dave pulled it up beside my ear anyway just like a legal executioner would have done.

Oh, Lordy Lordy!

My knees turned to water and I'd have fallen if I hadn't been held upright. As it was . . . okay, the truth was that I could feel a flood of wet heat down inside my britches, and it wasn't the rain that caused that.

They had the rope pulled so tight I could feel the way the wind was making the limb above me dance and jump.

"Look, damn you—" I started in to say.

Before I could get any more than that out, the one called Cap nodded and said something and Dave and two other guys started to pull.

The rope tightened around my throat and my feet came off the ground, and—God—I could feel the rope tighten. I was still trying to gulp in air, except it was harder than ever now, and there was a pounding and roaring in my ears that I'd never heard nor felt before.

I tried to kick and struggle, but I was still tied high and low and couldn't do more than make the rope come tighter around me.

I remember that much.

And then nothing more.

✛ 5 ✛

I WAS ALIVE. Cold as the grave and soaked through to the skin. Hurting more than I'd ever hurt in all my days. Crick in my neck—I didn't wonder why—and could scarcely breathe.

But I was alive.

I hurt so bad I wasn't sure if I liked that or not.

But I was alive.

I tried to figure out how and why, but I couldn't. All I was sure of was that it was so. And that I was miserable.

I lay there, hands bound so tight I couldn't feel them, shivering and my teeth and jaw clattering from the cold and the pain, a terrible weight on my chest that felt like somebody'd dropped an anvil there.

But I was alive.

The storm was raging something awful above and around me. I could feel and hear that, all right. The rain had turned to sleet and I could feel a thin rime of soft ice on my face. Most of my face seemed numb, but I could feel the resistance of it when my eyelids blinked.

I tried to look around, but when I opened my eyes I just got water into them and couldn't see anything anyway.

I could hear the pine boughs thrashing overhead, but it was too dark to see them.

A funny thing was that even though I could hear all that going on, the trees creaking the way they will do when they sway and the limbs being tossed and twisted and the wind soughing loud through the needles, even though I could hear all that, I couldn't feel any movement from it.

The last I'd known before they hauled me up off the ground to hang, I could feel every bump and dip of the tree limb they'd put the rope over.

Now . . . there wasn't any of that. Not the least bit of feeling.

The rope was still around my neck. When I tried to move my head—Lordy, but that hurt, the pain sharp and bone deep—I could feel the tough hemp bristly against my ear and the side of my head. So the rope was still there, and the wind was worse than ever and I sure would've thought I'd be able to feel all that thrashing and tearing, but I didn't. Not a bit of it.

Couldn't see anything either to help me figure out why.

Or why I was still alive.

Not that I was complaining. Not about that anyway.

But, God, I was so awful cold. I hadn't been wearing a coat or anything when they came at me like that. The evening had been fair and warm enough at the time, and I'd been sitting there by a good fire. I'd been just in my shirt-sleeves, with my vest unbuttoned and coat laid beside my saddle.

Now everything I had on was sopping wet, so that I tried to shrivel up and crawl deeper inside my skin, but I couldn't move anywhere to try and escape the cold or the wet.

I lay there, shivering and chattering and almost wishing I was dead. Almost. But not quite.

Because I was alive.

They'd hanged me, damn them, but I was alive.

I had no notion how. No idea why.

But I was alive.

I figured to stay that way if ever I could.

✛ 6 ✛

I SLEPT.

I wouldn't've thought that possible, but I guess it was so, because even though I wasn't really aware of dropping off, I found of a sudden that the sky was getting light and that there was a thin covering of snow over me.

The snow was a blessing really, as it kept in some of my body heat—what little there was of it—and kept some of the cold air off me.

The wind had died sometime during the night, must've been after I fell asleep, and I suppose that's when the rain and sleet turned to snow.

I wanted to wipe the moisture out of my eyes and off my face but of course couldn't, my hands and feet still being tied tight. Knowing that made my nose and left ear start to itch too. And my neck still hurt so bad it like to brought tears into my eyes.

I could see now, though, what happened and why I felt that heavy weight on my chest. There was a thick tree limb, the same one the rope was thrown over, lying on top of me. It must have given me some shelter through the night, although I hadn't realized it at the time.

Now the broken branch was lying half across me, the tufts of green needles dusted with snow and a smell of sap strong in the air. I hadn't particularly noticed that before, but now that I could see the branch I could smell it too. Funny how the senses will work like that.

Not that I was laughing. I was still in a helluva fix.

Could've been worse, though, and that is for certain sure.

Apparently, what happened was that those SOBs strung me up and tied the rope off and then rushed to jump onto their horses and get the hell off that mountain before the weather got worse.

Either my weight on the bough or maybe the whipping of that high wind was too much for the brittle wood to bear, and the branch broke and came down atop me.

I was too far gone to feel or know it at the time, but that saved me. That and the fact that they'd used an ordinary loop in the catch rope to put around my neck, so that the hondo let the rope slip loose once the weight was off it, plus the fact that they'd pulled me off my feet instead of dropping me off something, a horse's back or whatever.

In a proper hanging, it's not strangulation that does for a fellow but the snapping of his neck. That is the purpose of the hangman's noose. It is formed with those thick coils—thirteen is traditional but doesn't matter so far as the function is concerned—so as to make a thick, chunky lump. The bulky knot is positioned just behind the victim's ear. Then, when he hits the end of the drop, the rope is pulled straight and the knot snaps sideways. It pops the poor fellow's head right off the top of his spine. Death is instant and painless. Or so the hangmen claim, although just exactly how they come by this knowledge is something that I've yet to hear explained.

The reason the hangman is so careful about weighing and measuring his victim is to get the length of drop just right. More weight means less drop is needed or t'other way around for a light fellow. The trick is to make that knot perform sharp and strong enough to break the neck and cause immediate death but not so hard as to snatch the man's head off his body.

Not that I suppose the dead guy gives much of a damn, but it is embarrassing as hell to the hangman. Shows poor preparation and performance of the job, don't you see.

Crowds assembled for public hangings tend to get a first-class kick out of it, though. Not that it happens so awful often, but a head does come off every now and then, which may partly explain why executions are so uncommon popular.

Me, I would admit that I've watched a few public hangings my own self from time to time, though I never aspired to be the center of attention at one. And liked it all the less now that I'd had a taste of the experience.

I lay there, shivering and cold but not so bad as before, and thought about such things while I watched the light strengthen and eventually the sun creep up past the horizon.

What I was doing more than anything else, I suppose, was putting off my next worry, that being: Now that I was awake and alive, what the hell was I going to do about getting myself loose so I could *stay* that way?

The notion was appealing, but I hadn't the least idea of how to go about it.

✢ 7 ✢

As the sun climbed higher and the air began to warm, the snow melted, so that I was more conscious of being wet and cold.

And aside from the unscratchable itches that pestered and prodded at me, I started to get hungry. Now, if anybody'd gone and asked me before all of this happened, I would've thought that my stomach grumbling and gurgling would've been about the last thing a body would think of in a circumstance like this. But the truth was that I was plenty damned hungry, and the more my belly groaned, the madder about it I got.

There I'd been, minding my own business, laying out beside the fire for what I thought would be a nice, quiet night. And what happens? Some sons of bitches come along and hang me!

Annoying, it was, I tell you true.

I guess what was happening was that my empty stomach was reminding me that this morning I *was* still alive, damn them, and laying there cold and wet wasn't going to do anything toward the everyday requirements of my own mortal self.

So I'd best . . . what?

I squinted against the glare of the sun and scooched

around as best I could underneath that downed tree limb trying to figure out what was what so that maybe, just maybe, I could fashion some ideas toward the future.

Getting loose of all the ropes that were binding me seemed a pretty fair place to make my start on it.

My hands were tied, my feet were tied, and the noose around my neck was tangled up in the fallen pine branch and led eventually over to the bole of another, smaller tree where they'd tied it off so as to keep me suspended in the air. Or so they thought and intended. The rope was still tied there, of course, which meant that I was tethered to that tree in addition to everything else.

All in all I'd had better prospects.

But then, when you think about it, I'd sure had worse ones too. As recently as a matter of mere hours back.

A knife would've come in handy. But my knife was now in the pocket of one of the possemen. Oh, I remembered him just fine, thank you. Ugly SOB he was, in a calfskin vest and sleeve garters and a ratty old black hat that he probably got for a nickel after the first three owners got done with it. Yeah, I remembered him plain.

I didn't have my knife nor my wire cutters—nor, I saw when I craned my aching neck and peered over in that direction, anything else of the gear I'd come here with. Far as I could tell from where I lay, they'd gathered it all up and carried it off.

How the hell long had I been hanging there anyway for them to've gotten so much done? Lordy, I reckon it *was* a wonder that I wasn't dead.

Still, thinking about that wasn't getting me cut loose from the ropes, so I tried to quit dwelling on it and to think instead about something constructive.

Like . . . what is the next best way to sever a rope if you don't have a knife to hand?

The answer to that seemed simple enough, so I wriggled and scooted and flopped around some until I was most of the way out from under the fallen branch and could sit upright.

I took a close look at the ground around me, shifted position some more, and then leaned back against a flat rock the size of a saddle blanket and maybe ten, twelve inches thick.

It should do, I figured. Would pretty much have to, as it was the only one close to me that had a sharp edge to it.

Once I got myself situated the best I could manage, I commenced to rock back and forth, pushing down with my arms so as to drag that rope back and forth across the rough edge of the rock as I moved my body just like I was sitting in a creaky old front-porch chair.

Didn't seem to be accomplishing all that much.

But then, what the hell. It wasn't like I was going anywhere, so I was free to take all the time there was.

✢ 8 ✢

I THINK MAYBE the nicest thing I've ever felt—well, close to it anyhow—was when my hands came free. There wasn't any warning. I'd long since gotten scared that the damn rope wouldn't ever wear through. Got over that, more or less, by realizing that it just plain *had* to else I was dead meat just waiting to cool down. Anyway, I sat there rubbing slow and steady, if only for lack of a better plan, and eventually—I've no idea how long it took—I felt a sort of lurch and heard a very tiny little sound, and darned if I wasn't loose. At the hands anyway, and that was the most critical thing.

The first thing I did, I mean the very first, was to snatch that loop of rope off my neck. It had long since worked itself loose, wasn't tight at all, and shouldn't have been bothersome.

Well, let me tell you. It was bothersome. Just knowing the noose was there was bothersome. It annoyed me all to hell and gone, and I wanted it off of me and right dang *now*!

I pulled it off and with a grimace and a shudder tossed it aside.

What I took off couldn't have weighed more than a few ounces.

It felt like I'd gotten rid of the weight of the world. I breathed easier once it was gone, I guaran-damn-tee.

Next thing was to shove the fallen tree limb off me so I could sit up and untie my feet.

Once that was done . . . I just laid there.

Oh, I wanted to get up and move around. You bet I did. But I couldn't. After laying there cold and wet the whole night through, I was so stiff and stove up that I couldn't hardly make my muscles move. Couldn't get my feet under me and upright. Apparently, this recovery thing was gonna have to come slowly by degrees and never mind what my personal preference might've been.

So I sat there for a time. Taking deep breaths. Flexing my arms and fingers, working my toes up and down, drawing my legs up—they'd only move a little way to start with but gradually I was able to bring them higher—and waving my arms about. Good thing there wasn't anybody around to see or they'd've thought sure I was some kind of lunatic.

Of course, if there'd been anybody around to see, there would've been somebody I could turn to to light a fire and bum some beans and bacon off of.

I thought about that and realized that if there really had been anybody around way up here in the nowhere places, then it most likely would've turned out to be one of those damned possemen, and I'd've been in the soup all over again because of it.

Considering that as a possibility, maybe it wasn't so awful bad that I was alone up here after all.

Anyway, I sat there, stiff and shivering, and gradually warmed up a bit as the movement helped put some life back into my muscles and as the sun came higher and higher.

It was turning off a clear day and a fairly warm one despite the nasty weather overnight.

It was, in fact, a pretty damned good day to be alive, and I counted myself fortunate to be there breathing in that crisp mountain air and enjoying that bold sunshine.

Life, I thought, would be pretty good if only I had a horse. Or some food. Or . . . some-damn-thing.

✛ 9 ✛

THEY'D CLEANED ME out. Those decent, law-abiding, God-fearing, good-citizen possemen had taken everything I owned in this world.

Not just the money. I could almost've understood and forgiven them that, considering that they seemed to really think I'd stolen it from some payroll in whatever stupid little nothing of a town they came from. And if I couldn't actually forgive it, well, I could at least understand it.

But no, they weren't satisfied with taking the money they thought was theirs. They took *every*thing.

My horse was gone, of course. And the saddle that I'd owned and been comfortable on since I was—what?—fifteen years old maybe.

My saddlebags. Guns. Every damned thing I owned in this world had been picked up and carried off with them.

My boots. That, I think, was the cruelest blow of all. That scrawny, filthy, pale-haired bastard had taken my boots. But I thought I remembered . . . yes, over there. He'd tossed his old, used-up ones aside. I could see them lying half-hidden under a runty scrub oak a dozen feet or so away.

I got to my feet, spry as any eighty-year-old and aching in more places than I'd known I had, and limped across the rocks and gravel to gather up those cast-off boots and carry them back to where I could sit down on a more or less chair-high boulder. Getting down to ground level and back up again didn't seem a very good idea at the moment, what with the way my muscles were feeling.

I wiped the bottoms of my socks free of gravel and other such trash—it was a wonder the son of a bitch hadn't taken those too, him being barefoot inside his own boots—and pulled those nasty, smelly, cracked-leather abominations onto my aching feet.

Dang things were a tight squeeze, being a size or so smaller than was proper to fit me. But bad boots are better than no boots, let me tell you. A far sight better.

It helped considerable that the seams along the sides of both boots were split out and torn, because that relieved some of the tightness and made it bearable for me to wear them.

I wiggled and settled them as best I could and then stood up and stomped the ground a few times. They would do. And they sure felt better than being barefoot on that cold, moist ground.

That, though, was about all they'd left behind. Unless you count cold ashes.

Damned thieves hadn't even left me any live coals to make a fire with. And I needed fire awful bad. I was cold to the bone and still wet, and of course my coat and slicker were gone along with everything else I owned.

I needed a fire. I needed some hot food in my belly. No, let me amend that. I needed food in my belly. It would be nice to have something hot, but just to have something . . . most anything . . . would've taken me a long way down the road toward feeling better.

I needed those things, and I needed a coat. Blanket. Horse.

I needed a gun, dammit.

And I needed my money back.

First things first, though.

I sat there in my new-old boots and commenced to thinking about how to go about managing a fire and something to eat.

✠ 10 ✠

THE FIRE . . . I figured I could cope with that. Wouldn't be easy, but it would be possible. So I set to poking around to see what I could find.

Dry wood. That was the first and foremost, and inside clumps of scrub oak was the place to find it. There's always old, dead, dry trash underneath a thicket of the low-growing mountain scrub oak, and up here was no exception to that rule.

I first gave the sky a suspicious eyeballing, but bad as the night had been, the day was that clear and pretty. Dang sky was almost mocking in its cheerfulness it was so blue and nice. It had that "who me?" sort of innocence to it, like the meek look a cat will give you when you wonder why the finch's cage is empty.

Anyhow it sure looked safe enough to bring dry stuff out into the open now, so I went ahead and gathered what was going to have to pass as kindling. The dry and shriveled old leaves and tee-nincy bits of twigs would do fine for that, although I'd need something smaller and easier to light than that for tinder.

Still, I had some ideas about where to find myself some tinder, and sure enough, fifteen or twenty minutes of rooting around in the rocks—with a stick, thank you, not my bare hands, lest there be some pygmy rattlesnakes deep inside those holes—I came up with exactly what I wanted. A mouse nest. That fist sized mass of grass stems and leaf veins was old, dry, and perfect. I dragged it out intact and carried it back to where I figured to make my fire.

By this time it was coming late in the morning and my belly was grumbling and fussing for food, but fire was the first thing I needed, for I wasn't entirely sure I'd be able to make it if I had to spend another night all cold and wet. A man could take the ague and come down with the epizoodical shakes if he couldn't get warm and dry after so long, and you never knew what night could bring in these mountains. Another storm like last night's just might finish me if I didn't have a fire to huddle by, so my bellyaching belly was just going to have to wait its turn.

Once I had my tinder and kindling to hand, I scrounged up an old, long-ago fallen limb—easy enough to find—that was big enough to do the job I wanted but small enough that I could smash it over a rock to split it open and get a more or less flat slab of dry wood to work with.

I concentrated next on the scrub-oak thickets again, rooting and busting inside them like a grumpy old bear in search of acorns, until I found some sticks that were straight enough to do the job I wanted.

All of that occupied half the dang day, but it was time I had to spend, like it or not.

Eventually I got together all the things I thought I needed and sat down to unravel one of the short pieces of rope that had been used to tie my feet. I needed a stout cord but not so thick as that rope had been. Turned out that a quarter of the strands was just about right.

With the cord and one of my lengths of tough, nearly straight oak I made a bow.

The other length of oak, straighter and not quite so thick, I rubbed against the rocks until one end was more or less pointed and the other more or less flat. More or less was going to have to do on both ends, because precision just wasn't in the cards without the proper tools to work with. And if I'd had proper tools, dang it, I wouldn't have been going through all this primitive nonsense to begin with.

Anyway, once all of that was put together . . . shee-oot. Once all that was put together, I truly, fully, and properly appreciated whoever it was that invented the common sulfur-tip match.

I put everything in order. Kindling close to hand. Tinder crushed almost to powder—the mouse wouldn't have approved, but that was its hard luck and my good—and deposited inside a protected little hollow of stone. Softwood slab laid over the tinder so that any curly little wisps of hot coals would fall onto the tinder.

And me leaning my weight over top of the whole she-bang so I could get some serious friction onto the slab when I twirled that drill with the help of the bow.

They say it's possible to do this without the bow, using just a fellow's hands, but that sounded like it would take more patience—and, more to the point, more stamina—than I had left in me.

After that, well, it was just a matter of sawing back and forth, the fire-drill spinning inside the slack loop of my bowstring until the heat built intense enough to give me the start on a fire.

That and a *whole* lot of time and effort.

Yessir, I've no idea who the man was that first thought up the sulfur match, but I surely do thank and admire him.

✤ 11 ✤

GOD, IT FELT good to have a fire. And just think, it hadn't taken me but most of the dang day to make it.

Still, it was time mighty well spent. I built that sucker up until it was big enough to cook an elk on. Whole. And if I didn't have any meat to cook, I sure had myself to toast and dry out.

I wasted way too much wood to begin with, but I wanted that fire big. I wanted the warmth of it. I wanted my clothes dry. And I damn well wanted to know that I could make it through the coming night warm no matter what.

Between toastings, I'd dash out into the woods around about and gather more downed, dry wood so I'd be sure and have a plentiful supply overnight.

I stashed my fire drill and some more tinder under a rock to make sure they would be handy—and dry—in case another storm came up through the night, but in truth I wasn't much expecting more trouble. Not of that sort anyway. And if there wasn't any rain to dampen the coals, there would be heat enough in my fire pit to start a new blaze in the morning even if the fire did go out during the night.

My next need, now that I had warmth and dry clothing, was something to put into my belly.

Hungry? Worse than merely. I was ready to chew grass and swallow stones.

Yessir, what I wanted next was to find something to cook.

I picked up some likely-looking rocks and tried knocking a pine jay out of a tree, as that seemed a sensible plan if not necessarily a tasty one should I somehow manage to succeed.

Actually I needn't have worried about what one of those loudmouth jays would taste like. I used the best throwing stone I could find, took a windup and extra-careful aim . . . and missed the damn tree, never mind the bird that was sitting in it. It wasn't any wonder, I guess, that the other kids never wanted me on their baseball team when we'd play in the school yard those long years back. Pitching rocks just wasn't going to put meat onto the skewer.

I sure did salivate when I looked at the birds around me, though. And the more so when I'd spot a coney, one of those rabbitlike critters with the short ears and rock-dwelling habits.

What with the unraveled rope that I'd already used once to make my fire drill, I had the makings for some snares. About all my life I've heard tales about people, little kids even, catching game like conies and birds and stuff by setting snares for them in the brush.

Sounded like a heckuva idea. Except for one small detail. I didn't have the least idea how to go about making a dang snare. You used a loose-loop sort of thing. I knew that much, for I'd seen illustrations in a book sometime in the past. But what else you did with it apart from just dangling it off a twig or something, well, I hadn't any notion about that.

Snares, I figured, weren't apt to be my salvation.

I made my supper—which at the same time served as breakfast and lunch, as I hadn't eaten a thing the whole day long—by finding a puddle of rainwater in a depression atop a boulder and slurping that up like a stray dog drinking out of a mud puddle.

It wasn't dignified, I suppose. But that cold water in my belly felt almighty satisfying, everything considered. Yes, it did.

It was coming night by then, and I was tired. But in a strange way kinda satisfied. After all, I'd survived. I was still alive, and if I was hungry, well, I was nonetheless warm now and dried off and feeling better than I probably had any right to.

I drank up every last bit of water I could get off of that rock, added yet more wood to my bonfire, and stretched out on the bare earth to see could I manage to get a little sleep this night.

✛ 12 ✛

A LITTLE SLEEP? I slept like I was practicing at being dead. And felt pretty good when I woke up too. No longer tired, no longer cold, and the funny thing was that I was no longer tormented by being hungry.

Not that I wasn't wanting to eat. I was. But it wasn't deviling me so bad as it had the whole day before. It was kind of like my stomach had given up on the expectation of me putting anything into it and didn't want to bother with the nuisance of hunger pangs anymore.

On the other hand, now that I had the knowledge, I wasn't particularly eager to repeat this experiment of going for days in a row without eating. Once was plenty, thank you.

Anyway, I wasn't all that worried now about how to put some meat into my belly. I'd woken up already knowing how to manage that.

It had come to me in the night, and the funny thing was where it came from.

Sunday school. Would you believe it? It was a Sunday-school lesson that showed me how I could get something to eat.

And yes, there'd once been a time when I went to Sunday school. Got all dressed up in a fresh-boiled shirt and short pants with stockings up past my knees and went meek as a lamb off to Sunday school just like one of the good kids. Which I won't claim actually to've been my own self, but I was a lot closer to it then than in more recent times.

Anyway, I woke up knowing just exactly what I needed to do next, and promptly set about doing it.

First thing, I took some dry twigs and stirred through the ashes of last night's fire to locate some live coals buried in them, then quickly got a new fire to crackling. That took the chill off the morning air and added to my good humor.

Next I found me some flat rocks and smashed a few until I got a piece the size I wanted and with one of the freshly broken edges sharp enough to do a little cutting. It wasn't a knife, of course, but it would do.

I took up some more of the short rope lengths that I'd been hog-tied with and unraveled one of them to make smaller strands. Those weren't quite as long as I wanted, so I tied two together to make one cord of what seemed a likely length. Did that twice so as to have a pair of them.

Then I took my left boot off and, using the stone knife I'd made, began sawing and ripping at the cracked and already half rotten old leather on the upper part of the boot.

This whole deal was crude and haphazard, I suppose. But the truth is that I wasn't much interested in how it was going to look.

The proof of this pudding would be in the eating. Literally so.

I bent to my work with a pretty good feeling about things. To the point that I found myself whistling a gay tune while I sawed away at that beat up old boot, I felt that good about being alive.

✣ 13 ✣

NOW I GOT to say that I wasn't very good with my weapon. Not right off. I had to practice with it some. But I'd heard enough about it back in Sunday school, like I said, and once the Sunday-school teacher, who was the town blacksmith the rest of the week, even gave a sort of demonstration using pieces of string and paper and, if I remember correctly, a stub of chalk as the missile.

Well, what I had was strong cord, supple leather, and some smooth, small stones.

Not exactly a proper hunter's sling like little David had maybe. But then it wasn't any giant I was setting out to kill either. Just some noisy old jays or, better yet, a coney. That was what I really wanted, rabbit meat being so tasty. I'd never had any jay to eat, so couldn't rightly comment about how they might taste. But the prospect wasn't very enticing. I'd naturally eat one if I brought one down, but it sure wouldn't be my first choice. To get either one, though, I'd first have to be able to hit it.

So I spent a half hour or so practicing swinging my sling around, whirling it so fast it hummed through the air, and then learning just when to let go of the one cord—one at a time only, as I learned once by mistake and sent the whole shebang flying through the air—so that my stone flew more or less true.

It was easier to get the hang of—pardon the expression—than I'd expected. And it wasn't like I had to worry about conserving ammunition. Heck, I was standing right on top of all the projectiles a fellow could ever want. All I had to do for a new one was bend down and pick one up. So I could practice to my heart's content and not worry about running out of objects to throw.

Of course it wasn't my heart I was trying to make content but my stomach, so the practice session only lasted long enough for me to see something to throw at. After all, I might as well learn by missing something edible as by throwing at a pinecone.

I threw at, and missed, enough birds to scare about all the rest of them away, but by then I was starting to get the feel of using a sling and stone, so went to sneaking around in the rocks along that mountaintop until I found a purely suicidal cony standing out where I could see him.

I wound 'er up, whipping that sling around and around until it was just a blur in the corner of my eye and a loud hum beside my ear, and when I let fly I nailed the furry little critter.

Truth is that I didn't exactly hit where I was aiming. My stone was off by a good foot or more. But it was traveling plenty fast and more by blind luck than any particular skill, when the stone bounced it hit the little varmint just underneath his eye and knocked him over slick as a Kewpie doll at a tent-show amusement booth.

Well, I went leaping and larruping over there quick, lest he only be momentarily stunned and gave his neck a brisk wring to make sure he wouldn't be getting away.

After that it was back to the fire and my stone knife.

Breakfast, by golly, was served.

✦ 14 ✦

WITH MY BELLY full—well, mostly; coneys are not very big but do taste just fine—I had the leisure to sit back and do some thinking about something other than simple survival for the next few hours.

It's funny how that works. But ever since I came around from my almost-but-not-quite demise I'd been too scared and busy to think of anything other than the basics of breathing.

Now, clean-picked bones roasting on the coals of a good fire, I was able to put my attention to other things.

Things like those sons of bitches who'd hanged me. And the five thousand dollars they'd carried off with them when they left.

I thought it over real careful, let me tell you. And the conclusion I came to was that I was really, truly, and deeply peeved with those old boys.

Seven of them, there'd been. A posse, they claimed. Posse nothing. They were a bunch of lowlifes. Hadn't any more right to hang me than they would've had a right to pickle and eat the corpse after.

So yeah, I was plenty peeved.

The question now was what I was gonna do about it.

Also what I *could* do about it, those two not necessarily following the same vein.

The most sensible thing, I soon enough recognized, would be to send up a chorus of hallelujiahs in sheer gratitude for still being alive and go the other way just as far and as fast as I could manage. Yessir, that would be the most sensible thing possible, considering that if I showed up alive where any single one of those fellows ever saw, they would likely want to rectify their past errors and not do such a sloppy job of hanging the second time around.

They did, after all, think that I stole their damned payroll money.

But the truth is that I hadn't. I really hadn't, dammit. I'd been telling them the natural truth when I denied taking their damned money.

Now, okay, I've been known to lie now and then. Yes, I have. But not this time.

And to be made out a liar when this time I was telling the damn truth, well, it irked me. It purely did.

Besides, I wanted to get back at them.

Think about it. They'd come at me, sneaking out of the night. Held me up with guns. Took every last lick of worldly goods that I possessed. And then did their level best to kill me on top of all that.

You better believe I was mad about it.

You better believe I wanted back at them for it.

Of course, I had no means to get at them. Had no horse. No gun. Didn't even know what stupid jerkwater town they came from.

All I had was a fire drill and a half-assed slungshot. And never mind that I'd brought down a critter to put in my belly, I was no David, and if those possemen weren't Goliaths either, there sure was more than just the one of them to make up for what they lacked in size.

So yeah, the right and proper and sensible thing for me to do was to just gather up my drill and slungshot and head off the other way.

Did I do that?

Not hardly.

I picked up my miserable few things and set off to follow the tracks of the horses those SOBs had ridden down off the mountain from that hanging tree.

I was going hunting. And this time not for no coney.

✢ 15 ✢

JUST TO CLARIFY a point, those handsome gray scrub jays are stringy and their meat is dark and there isn't very much of it on one of the critters, but they don't taste as bad as I might've expected. In fact, if a man is hungry enough they can taste kinda good. You can believe me on this subject because scrub jays provided my groceries for the next couple days, the best thing about them being that they are used to being camp robbers and deliberately come close around a fire or people. That makes them easy to knock down, especially after a little practice with the sling.

I liked the coney meat a whole lot better, of course, but they only live pretty high up and I left them behind and above me that first day.

Time I reached flat ground again—well, more or less flat—the jays and the trees they'd been sitting in were behind me too. Down below there was nothing but some tufts of dry, brown grass, and a lot of sunbaked ground surrounding them.

Back on the mountain it hadn't been so hard to see where the posse's horses had been, as the ground there was wet when they passed over it, and they left plenty of sign behind.

Down here on the flat my trailing luck ran out. The rain

must have ended before they got down this far.

I paused there at the foot of the mountain for a bit to ponder and to prepare for a dry and empty walk. I doubted I could find much in the way of firewood once I was out into open country, so I killed as many birds as I could in the last of the afternoon and cooked them while I had the chance.

Unfortunately, I was still plenty hungry and didn't feel I was getting all that much nourishment out of the jays, so I went and ate most of them before the night was through.

Time I was done with breakfast that next morning I only had three cooked birds to carry in my pack.

Pack? What for pack? Why, I was a traveling man, wasn't I, and a traveling man needs his possibles, doesn't he? Using rope and the vest I'd still been wearing—I figure they would have stolen that too except my hands were tied and they couldn't have pulled the vest off me without untying me to do it—I made a pouch sort of thing to carry my fire-making tools, the rest of the rope, and some dry mouse nests for tinder. And now, of course, my scrub-jay carcasses. Oh, I was a well-equipped traveler for sure.

So I gathered my scant few things together and slung the pack over one shoulder and my sling over the other and figured I was ready to strike out into the unknown.

Those seven men were out there somewhere.

I figured they had maybe half the damn territory to hide in.

I also figured that would not be anywhere near enough.

✢ 16 ✢

FACT IS, A bindlestiff wanderer can make out pretty good just by living off the land. Not that I'd recommend it, exactly, and not that I had been or was fixing to do such a thing deliberately. But it wasn't near as bad as I might've expected it to be.

Even out on the desert it turned out I could find plenty enough to eat. No coneys or birds out there, of course, and I could see jackrabbits all around. They made me hungry just to look at them, but they were way too spooky to get within slungshot range. I never even got close enough to throw a rock at one.

No, the easily available food there turned out to be snakes. Rattlesnakes, if you want to be get specific about it.

I'd see half a dozen or more in a day's walking, and they were easy prey to the usual doubled-over coil of rope.

I learned soon enough to just put the slungshot away in my bag and carry a loop of rope in my hand ready to whip the rattlesnakes with.

Cut the head off so as to eliminate the fangs and poison—I've heard it said that a rattlesnake can kill you stone dead for days after it has been killed if you so much as scratch yourself with one of those fangs—and they cleaned up pretty decent. Just skin them out and lay them in a tight coil around a small fire and they'd cook up fine. Bony, of course, but it was kinda like eating a chicken neck except with more meat on it. They tasted considerable better than the scrub jays did.

At night I didn't have any real wood to make myself a lasting fire to keep me warm, so that was something of a problem. I could build enough fire to cook with just by piling up dry grass, but of course that doesn't last any time at all. A few minutes and all you have left is ashes. Not even any coals to use for making the next fire.

It was cold overnight, what with not having a blanket or even a coat to put on. But it was bearable. Just.

To guard against the rattlesnakes—I welcomed dead ones for food but sure didn't want to bunk in with any live ones, like having them crawl inside my pant legs for warmth as I'd heard of them doing sometimes—I just laid out my pieces of rope in an oval on the ground and lay down inside it.

They say a snake won't ever crawl across a grass rope. The theory is that the fibers of the hemp tickle their bellies. Now, I don't know if that's true or not, but I've known an awful lot of fellows who wouldn't think of laying out a bed on the ground without putting a grass rope around it. And I have to say that, when I did that there wasn't a single snake came around me overnight.

With those basic needs tended to, there was only one thing left that was truly worrisome, and that was water.

Lordy, but I was dry.

It wouldn't have been so bad, maybe, if I'd had something I could carry water in. That way I could have brought some along with me.

The best I could manage was to drink what blood I could out of the snakes I killed and chew the inside pulp of the few barrel cactuses that I came across. The cactus pulp wasn't wet but it was a tiny bit moist. And the stuff tasted like . . . well, never mind just exactly what it tasted like. Trust me. It wasn't ambrosia.

I was so dry my lips cracked and my tongue commenced to hurt. But I was alive and moving. That was the important part.

I wasn't entirely sure it was the tracks of that posse that I was following, but every so often, say every quarter to half a mile or thereabouts, I'd spot a fresh scrape on a caliche flat or once in a great while see part of a hoofprint. There were no guarantees that those were made by the horses I wanted to follow, but I had the idea that maybe they were.

And it wasn't like I had anyplace else to go and anything else to do in the meantime.

So I kept on walking and killing snakes and cussing more than a little, and on the afternoon of the third day since leaving the mountain behind—leaving it behind? I could still see it behind me looking like I'd hardly moved out of its shadow—I reached a rim overlooking as green and pretty a valley as I think I've ever seen.

I didn't have the least idea what this place was, but if it'd been up to me, I would've named it Paradise Oasis, for it surely looked to be both.

I found a rock to sit and rest on for a while and just sat there looking down into that lush and pretty place.

✛ 17 ✛

THERE WAS WATER down there. I couldn't see it. Not
directly. But I could see plain enough that it had to be
there, and in right fair amount too.

The valley was strung out long and lean, starting underneath a pair of loaf-shaped buttes to my left a couple miles
off—to the west that would be and north—and running east
by a bit south until it opened out onto dry, brown desert
away out to my right somewhere.

Down inside the walls that contained it on the north and
south sides, there had to be a lot of subsurface water because there was aplenty of grass and in the middle a line
of actual trees strung out beside what surely would turn out
to be a creek that I couldn't see from up top.

At the far west end it looked like there were some walls
or cliff faces and just below them the ground was mostly
brown and dry. I was guessing that the water came out of
the buttes somewhere up in that area and then gradually
spread out as it seeped and ran down the valley floor. A
quarter mile or so out from those west end cliffs the lush
grass started.

Smack in the middle I could see the roofs of some town,
and the whole lower end of the valley was marked off in
what looked almost like checkerboard squares from up

above where I was. Farms, those would be. Darned if there weren't a bunch of small farms right out here in the middle of absolutely nothing and downright nowhere. Farms. Who would've thought it.

Above the town, which itself was mostly hidden inside the trees, the land was left to grass, and I could see livestock of some sort grazing there. Horses and cattle both.

They were pretty far off, but it's easy to tell a horse from a cow and vice versa even from afar, if you just remember that a grazing horse makes a rounded shape while a cow looks squared off at both ends.

On the far north wall and above the town—to the left or west of it, that is—there was a collection of big buildings, some of them built on top of the rim on that side and others strung out in a string coming down into the valley. There must have been half a dozen of them, not counting sheds and other small structures, and at the bottom there was a really big place with three smokestacks. Although where they'd find anything around here to burn puzzled me plenty because it was obvious they weren't cutting and using up all those trees. It took me a minute to work out that it must have been a mine of some sort. Apparently, they were digging some kind of ore out of the valley. What kind of ore, well, I didn't know nor particularly care.

But it did occur to me that a mining company might well be the sort of outfit that would carry a big payroll.

Like, say, five thousand dollars' worth of payroll.

I figured that I just might well have found the place those good old boys of the hanging posse came from.

With that in mind, damn them, I ate the last of my rattlesnake meat and started looking for a way down.

✛ 18 ✛

THERE WAS A switchback path snaking down the face of the south wall. The rock and gravel way was about a horse and a half wide and easy to negotiate. It had also been used fairly recently, making me think again that this could well be the place that I wanted.

I was about halfway down, out there completely exposed to view in the event anyone happened to be looking, when it occurred to me that finding the hanging posse just might not be completely unalloyed good fortune.

After all, what they'd done poorly the first time they might learn to do somewhat better a second time around.

I felt naked and kinda uncomfortable the rest of the way down, let me tell you. And my neck began to hurt again, although that had more or less subsided over the past couple days. Right up to then.

I got to say that I felt considerably better once I got down to level ground, where I'd have a shot at hiding if anyone should happen along.

Made it down intact, though, and promptly found myself another rock to perch on and do some thinking.

I hadn't actually thought about what I was going to do once I got there, but walking into town and making a spectacle of myself looked to be an extra-dumb way to commit suicide.

Anyone who would insist on it being a hanging offense for someone to have a wad of cash money on his person wasn't apt to wise up over the course of a meager few days. What they'd thought then they would just as likely continue to think now, and I wouldn't favor hanging a second time any the more if they went through the formalities of a trial.

What I needed to do was . . . well, I didn't exactly *know* what I needed to do. Yet.

What I did figure was that I needed to know more before I made any firm plans on the subject.

In the meantime I needed something to eat—there wouldn't likely be much in the way of rattlesnakes and scrub jays down inside the valley here—and ideally a gun to defend myself with.

After that . . . I wasn't entirely sure.

I suppose I had some half-formed notion to sneak around and identify the possemen—Lord knew I had the face of each man secure in my mind as firm as if I'd been presented with oil portraits of the sons of bitches—and then . . . I dunno. Get them off in private one by one and return the compliment they'd paid me up on that mountain.

Or something.

But for sure, I realized now, it would be plenty dumb of me to show myself in public before I at least got the lay of things.

That being the case, I decided it made sense to put first things first. Gun, food, maybe some clothes. Stuff to replace the stuff that'd been stolen from me.

So I turned down-valley and hung close to the south wall, staying out of sight while I went looking for a farmhouse to burglarize.

✦ 19 ✦

I PICKED THE last, most isolated farmhouse in the valley. It was built well away from the riverbed that ran through the middle, and fairly far off the subsurface water too, judging from the grass and the crops growing in the neatly fenced little squares of dirt that surrounded the house.

The plots south of the house, those furthest away from the water, were grass. And none too healthy a stand of it either. Better than prairie grass, of course, but not lush and thick like I'd been seeing toward the upper end of the valley. I guess this was about where the water ran out, for off to the east all I could see was brown and ocher and yellow just like the empty country I'd been walking through for these past several days.

North of the house the squares were given over to standing grain crops like oats and barley and a little ground was planted to corn, squash, and like that, everything fairly hardy when it came to needing water.

It was coming late in the day by then, but I could see a fellow—barely see him, for the top of his head was all that showed above the stalks—out hoeing between the corn-rows.

There were a few little Jersey cows using what grass there was. Pretty little things, Jerseys, if not big or beefy.

But like I said, mighty pretty. A Jersey has eyelashes that'd make a saloon girl swoon with envy and eyes to match.

They also give mighty rich and tasty milk, and if there is anything I like, it is milk. I know, rough and tough old rangeland hombres are supposed to like whiskey and beer and all that, and I do. In the proper time and place, if not to excess like some fellas do. But my preference most of the time is coffee, and my all time favorite treat for a beverage is milk. Love the stuff. Always have.

And here were these pretty little Jersey milk cows, five of them, with their bags hanging full and it coming on toward milking time. By the time I came near, the cows were already drifting on their own toward the barn that sat behind the farmhouse.

While I watched those five cows clomped and clattered through the enclosure that I guessed was supposed to be a little bitty feedlot, and then they went on inside the barn and out of sight.

It occurred to me that it wouldn't be safe for me to go inside and burgle that farmer's house until morning, when I could be pretty sure he would be staying out in his fields for the best part of the day. If I went in now he was like to come in for the evening and find me.

But if I slipped into his barn and took a little milk to tide me over through the night, well, there'd be no harm done to anyone.

I stood up tall and looked again, and the farmer was still busy in the corn patch.

The cows were in the barn.

There sure wasn't any traffic going by, as this place down here was pretty much the end of the line, with nowhere to go beyond it but dry desert.

And my belly was rumbling something pitiful now that I saw those cows and was thinking about milk. I could practically taste it already, and my mouth was running full with spit in anticipation of a big dipper of fresh, rich, fat-yellow Jersey milk. Yessir, I could as good as taste it already.

I stuffed my snake-killer piece of rope inside my traveling pouch along with the slungshot and moved over to where the house and barn were between me and the cornfield. Then, as bold as if I had every right in the world to be there, I marched over to the barn and those bag-full Jerseys.

✢ 20 ✢

THERE WERE TWO galvanized buckets hanging on pegs
on the front wall and a four legged stool set on the
ground below them. The buckets were clean inside and
out—I checked them careful—so I took one down and got
the stool, and by that time my mouth was running so full
in anticipation that I had to spit lest I get cramps and a
sour stomach from swallowing too much of my own saliva.

Let me make it plain. After several days of nothing but
rattlesnake blood and cactus pulp, the prospect of having
some milk to drink was almighty attractive to me, and I
was about as anxious for it as a man can get.

I carried the bucket and stool over to the nearest cow
and surveyed the situation.

The cow was small, like all Jerseys seem to be, and calm
enough. And it didn't have any horns, not that it seemed
inclined to hook me or kick or anything anyway. It turned
its head and gave me what I thought was a kinda skeptical
look out of those big, soft, brown eyes. But it didn't snort
or try to get away anywhere, so I set the stool down beside
her hindquarters and bent to put the bucket down under her
udder.

Darn cow took a couple steps away.

I picked up the bucket and the stool and went over beside her to try again.

Darn cow moved away. This time her nigh hind hoof tipped the bucket over before I could get it, and it fell over into what was left of a fresh cow pie after five cows had finished walking around over it. That made for a mess that I didn't want to drink out of, so I left the stool there and went to get the other bucket. The clean one.

When I came back the cow had moved again. The stool was sitting along in the middle of the barn floor and all the cows were lined up facing against a sidewall.

That confused me for a minute. Then I realized that the arrangement of boards that I saw over there wasn't a weird sort of fence but apparently was something a farmer uses to hold a cow's head still—and the rest of the critter in place—so he can milk it without the cow walking off or knocking over the milk bucket.

And if you've gotten the impression that I don't actually know much about the milking of cows, well, the truth is that I *don't* know much about the milking of cows. Never been a farmer. Never wanted to be one. Never spent much of my free time studying up on ways to hoe corn or milk cows or any of that farmer stuff.

But, like I'd suppose most everybody else, I'd seen a cow milked before. Couple of times, maybe. And how hard can it be, anyhow?

So I went over to where the cows were lined up and examined those vertical wood pieces and saw that they moved from side to side. Then a couple of the Jerseys stuck their heads through to a trough on the other side, and I figured out how this deal was supposed to work. They'd stand there and eat while the farmer took the milk. Fine.

I went and found a fork and climbed up to the loft to pitch some hay down, then carried that over to the trough and fed the dang cows. I was, I would admit, becoming just the least bit annoyed with all this nonsense. I'd never thought there would be so much involved when all I wanted to do was get me a quick quart of milk and then go hide someplace until morning.

Still, it had to be done if I wanted the milk. So I did it. Didn't pitch very much hay, though. I didn't want there to be any of it left over to tip the farmer that a milk rustler had been making free with his stuff. As for the dirty bucket, well, I'd worry about that later. Right now what I wanted was milk.

So I fetched the stool out of the middle of the floor and set it down close beside the cow at the near end of the line of them. Didn't want to squeeze in between them to where I might get kicked or something. Having to squat down and milk a cow was a humiliating enough idea without coming away from the experience with a bloodied nose too.

I got my bucket set just so and wriggled around on the stool a bit and contemplated the task before me.

Now, like I said, I've seen a cow milked before. Not often maybe. But I've seen it.

I knew enough to realize where the stuff comes from and to know that you take hold with both hands and . . . pull, I expect.

The cow is supposed to do the rest.

So I checked once again to make sure the bucket was where the milk should run into it. Took a deep breath.

And grabbed hold of the two near spigots.

Tight.

✠ 21 ✠

I EXPECT I'D done that just a wee bit wrong somehow. I wouldn't know exactly how, but the cow sure seemed to.

So I rubbed the sore place on my shoulder where she'd nailed me with that back hoof—cows kick *forward* with their back feet while horses kick backward, and I guess I'd kinda forgotten that—and got up off the ground.

The bucket had gone flying even further than I did, and now there were two buckets that weren't clean enough to drink out of. In fact this one was worse than the first, so I got the first one again and figured I'd just drink out of the one side of it that didn't have any mess on it.

I also made the mistake, though, of wiping my britches off as I'd landed hard on my backside. Did it without thinking about it and came away with a wet and smelly handful. So I had to take some time to grab a wad of sweet-smelling soft hay and clean myself a mite.

This farmering business was not a career I would personally aspire to, I very quickly decided.

The cow was standing there chewing hay just as calm and quiet as you please through all this, darn her.

I guess I sighed a little and gave the miserable creature a dirty look. But I still wanted that milk and she still had it, so I picked up the stool once again and that more or less clean bucket and went back at 'er.

I am a lot of things, I will admit, and a good many of them bad, but the word "quitter" isn't to be found anywhere on that list.

I got my stuff placed to my liking—and hoped it was all to the cow's liking too—and tried again. But this time I spoke to her and rubbed her some, like you will do with a strange horse you want to saddle, and she didn't kick.

This was more like it.

I took hold of the handles—gently and careful this time, thank you—and pulled. Not too hard. Just kinda . . . polite.

The cow took in another mouthful of hay and paid no mind to me.

Didn't drip any milk into the bucket either.

I tried again. Harder this time. The cow stamped one foot and seemed a tiny bit annoyed, but there still wasn't any milk coming out.

I pulled and tugged and started to get more than a little bit hot under the collar, to the point that I was grumbling and cussing out loud, and if that cow had understood what I was saying she would've been purely scandalized.

But no matter how hard I yanked or from what angle, all that happened was that the cow stood there eating hay and swishing her tail and that bucket sat on the ground empty as a politician's promise.

I was starting to get really, really mad about this deal.

And then I heard somebody start laughing.

✝ 22 ✝

"YOU DON'T REALLY have to work for your supper, you know." She laughed again, louder this time. "And if you do insist on working, please try doing something you know about. You're making poor Lou upset."

"Lou?"

"The cow. Those are Lou Cow, Moo Cow, Blue Cow . . . you don't really want to know all this, do you?"

I shook my head. I didn't know if that was the right thing to do or not. The truth was that I was confused. Very. Lou Cow? Good grief!

And how do you tell if a cow is upset anyway? Far as I could tell, the stupid thing was just standing there chewing. It didn't look very upset to me.

Neither, fortunately, did the woman. She came into the barn—she'd been standing at the doorway, only about half-visible—and I got a better look at her. She was somewhere in her middle to late twenties, I thought. Spare and dry and going fast to wrinkles the way farm women do. Her face was tanned, her hair covered over with a towel or something wrapped completely around her head. She was tall and strode right on out, not prissing around or walking like she was being watched by some muck-a-muck. No nonsense about her.

I suppose I should have given thought to there being a woman in the house. It's just that I never considered that a woman would be the one to come out and do the milking.

Caught me fair and square, she did. Of course the good thing was that she didn't know that she'd caught me trying to steal the milk. She thought I was wanting to work for it. I didn't intend to disabuse her of that notion either.

She motioned me away from the stool and the bucket and the cow and the frustrations that went along with the them, and I was glad enough to oblige. When I stood, though, I got something of a surprise. I'd seen before that she was tall for a woman, but I hadn't realized just how tall. When I stood up, my knees popping only a little bit, I had to look *up* just a little to look into her eyes.

I couldn't remember ever before meeting a woman taller than me. Not that I'm so awful tall, mind, but women most generally are on the short side. Except for this one.

She had strange eyes too. Not weird or anything. But strange. Gray, you might say, or maybe blue—the end-of-day light wasn't so awfully good inside that barn—but so pale it was like they hadn't any color at all. When you looked at them, all you really saw was these little black dots in the middle, whatever you call those. Strange.

It took me some aback looking at her eyes. I don't really know why.

I guess I stood there tongue-tied for a couple seconds, just sort of staring, and she prodded me in the upper arm and nodded. "Move aside and let me, will you?"

"Yes, ma'am." I moved aside and let her.

She spread the skirts of her dress wide and hunkered down on that stool just like a man would, then mumbled something to the cow and rubbed the animal's flanks and then the heavy bag.

"You have to let them know that everything is all right," she said. As if I really wanted to know how to milk a dang cow.

"And you don't pull the milk out. You push it. Here. Lean down here. I'll show you."

I bent down beside her to where I could see. I could smell something—salt maybe? I wasn't sure—on her when I was that close.

"Now, see what I'm doing."

She took a handful of cow and squeezed.

"Start from the top. See that? And work down one finger at a time to push the milk out. Watch now."

She did it like that and there was a squirt of fresh, frothy milk that hit the bottom of that steel bucket so hard it made a thin, ringing sound.

"And now this hand. Then this one. See how I'm doing it?"

Be danged. It worked. She was doing that squeezing thing—not pulling really, though from a distance off it looked like it was pulling—and now there was milk squirting one side and then the other.

"And you can't forget the other tits." She leaned a little closer, pressing her cheek against the cow's flank so she could reach under to the other side of the bag, and milked that pair too.

It made me more than a little uncomfortable to hear a lady use that kind of language, though. I mean, there wasn't anything wrong with it. It was a right and proper word for the, uh, item concerned. But I guess I'd never heard a woman use words like that before. Not a decent woman anyway.

I felt some heat come into my face, but the woman didn't look in my direction, so it was all right.

I stayed where I was, leaning close and watching. She hadn't told me to do otherwise. She kept right on milking. She filled that bucket almost full, then brushed me away—I was able to straighten up finally and felt something of a crick in my back when I did—and went to get the other bucket. She made a sour face when she saw the mess I'd gotten onto her clean bucket.

"Here." She shoved the filthy bucket into my hands, dirt and all, which I didn't especially appreciate since she wasn't particular about giving me the dirty part to take hold of. "Clean this."

"Where . . ."

"The well, of course. Go draw water from the well—you do know what a well looks like, I hope—and wash this off. Do the best job you can because you will be drinking what I put into that bucket. Do you understand me?"

"Yes, ma'am."

"Fine. Now go do what I told you."

"Yes, ma'am."

Before I turned to go outside and find the well, I noticed she was emptying the first bucket into a big, tall metal can that I'd thought held grain or something. Instead it apparently was supposed to hold milk.

Well, that made sense enough, I supposed. Five cows and each of them giving more than a bucket of milk. It would take a powerful big family to get around that much milk, and I hadn't seen nor heard any crowd of kids around this place, so it was only reasonable there would be milk left over to be sold or swapped.

I got busy with my chores—so to speak—and wondered while I did what it was the woman with the strange eyes would be cooking for supper.

She *had* said something about supper, I seemed to recall.

Getting caught, I was thinking, was like to turn out even better than stealing some milk would have done.

✠ 23 ✠

"YOU CAN SET that pitcher onto the table if you please, Mr. . . . . what is your name, anyway?"

I set the heavy milk jug onto the table like she wanted but didn't say anything.

The woman wasn't going to let it go at that. "I believe you were going to tell me your name?" she prodded.

"Wesley," I said. "Wes for short. Last name is Johnson."

"Thank you, Mr. Johnson." She went on with setting the table.

Wesley Johnson. I was going to have to remember that, at least for a little while.

I have no idea where the name came from. I mean, I've never in my life known anybody named Wes or Wesley. Not that I can recall. Johnson, though, Johnson I've always liked. It's common but not so much so that it sounds suspicious, like Smith or Jones.

Besides, a man calling himself John Smith shows a lack of imagination and always makes me think he's a little bit light in the thinking department. I have more pride than that myself.

I noticed the woman was putting out only two of everything. Two plates, two cups, two spoons, two knives, like that.

"Won't we be waiting for your husband, ma'am?"

"It would be a long wait, Mr. Johnson. I'm a widow. And my name is Mrs. Kaufman."

"I'm sorry, ma'am."

"Sorry that my name is Kaufman, Mr. Johnson?" She looked up from the table and gave me this deadpan look, but there was a sparkle in those odd, pale eyes that belied the expression.

I couldn't help it. I started out to roaring with laughing and kept it up until my belly hurt and I had to drag a stool out from under the table and sit on it. It was either that or fall down. And even then I kept on laughing.

Mrs. Kaufman, I noticed, hadn't taken offense. To the contrary, she was laughing right along with me.

"It wasn't all that funny, Mr. Johnson," she said when I was in a condition to pay attention again.

"No, ma'am, I suppose it wasn't, but it sure struck me that way anyhow." I chuckled a little more and wiped my eyes. "You don't know what I been through lately."

"How is that, Mr. Johnson?"

"I've been walking, ma'am. Managed to get lost somehow and been walking. Eating snakes and like that. It's been . . . interesting."

"I wondered, of course, how you ended up all the way down here. Most people come into the valley by the road. They go direct to the mine looking for work or they stop in town first."

"Ma'am, I haven't seen a road in more than a week." Which was the natural truth.

She made a face. "Snakes! Really?"

"Really."

"No wonder you're hungry, Mr. Johnson."

"I will admit that the thought of real food is kinda attractive, ma'am."

"I'll have it on the table in a few minutes," she promised.

I wondered could I help myself to a cup of the milk first but decided to do the polite thing and keep my hands off until she joined me. It was just as well that I waited, because Mrs. Kaufman was one of those that likes to pray over food before she bites into it.

She saw that I was minding my manners, though, and was nice enough to hurry up and take a seat quick so as to get the praying out of the way, then she poured some of that fresh, frothy milk into my cup and told me to enjoy it while she put everything else onto the table.

Lordy, but that milk did taste fine. I drank it and three more cups of it before she could get things moved from the stove to the table.

Turned out that Mrs. Kaufman was a frugal sort, although whether that was by choice or not I couldn't know. Supper consisted of rice with milk gravy on it, some biscuits light enough that they needed gravy too lest they float right off the plate, and some sort of sweet jam that wasn't like anything I'd ever tasted before. No meat, though. Not that I was complaining. Not hardly.

I commented on the jam.

"Do you like it, Mr. Johnson? I make it myself. Cactus blossom. Every spring when the cactus bloom out in the basin"—she nodded toward the east, out into the empty land away from this valley where the water was—"I go out to collect the buds. They're tasty, don't you think?"

"Yes, ma'am, I surely do." It was no lie.

"I hope you don't mind doing without meat."

"No, ma'am, not at all." Now, that part was a lie of sorts. I mean, it was good to have real food again and anything would have been more than acceptable to me. But I surely do like my red meat too.

"I tried raising chickens when we . . . when I first came here, but that didn't work out very well. What the coyotes and foxes didn't get, the owls and eagles did. My flock didn't last very long. I haven't tasted an egg since. Eggs are the one thing that I really miss."

"Yes, ma'am. There's nothing like an egg, that's for sure." Or better yet the hen that laid it. Fried with the skin all crispy. Or cooked up with a mess of dumplings. A woman who could make biscuits like these would surely make a mean dumpling too, I was thinking. But I didn't say anything, figuring Mrs. Kaufman might be one of those odd folk who don't eat any meat. It's a religious thing with them, or so I'm told, though I can't claim to understand it my own self. And I'd already seen that the lady was a religious sort, praying before her meal and everything.

"Tell me, Mr. Johnson."

"Yes, ma'am?"

"Are you any better handling a hoe than you are a cow's teat?"

"I couldn't be much worse at it, could I?" I said with a grin.

She laughed. "No, you really couldn't."

I knew what would be coming on the heels of a question like that and gave it a moment's thought.

It wouldn't hurt for me to have a place down here in this valley where I could sleep and eat and stay out of sight while I worked out what I wanted to do next.

And the food was good even if there wasn't any meat. I reached for the rice and the gravy boat and waited for the lady to try and talk me into helping her out around the place.

KNOW WHY I never wanted to be a farmer? Because it's work, dang it. It even makes you *sweat*. Shee-oot, ma'am, no thank you.

But under the circumstances . . .

I got right out there in the hot sun and whacked weeds until I was sweating as good as a professional farmer could've.

Not that I can for the life of me figure out how a weed would manage to grow in ground like that. Why, you'd think there wouldn't be any way some weak little old sprig of a weed could force its way through the surface of that soil. Dang ground was hard as kiln-baked brick. I know, 'cause along with chopping the weeds—and there were sure plenty of them and then some—me and my hoe were having to bust up the ground and loosen it. *Aerate* it, Mrs. Kaufman called it, whatever that means.

I think a cold chisel and maul would've been better tools for the job than a flimsy little hoe. But then what the heck do I know about farming? Done with that one? Now ask me how much I *want* to know about farming. Huh!

I was learning, though. Oh yes, I was learning.

She got me started in to whacking weeds just after breakfast. And breakfast came just before daybreak. This woman was as hard driving a boss as any trail-drive foreman there's ever been. Harder than most.

I will say that she wasn't one to shirk her own self, though. First she showed me what needed doing and how to do it, then she went off to the barn to do the morning milking. Soon as that was done she came back out to the corn patch with a second hoe in hand. She went to chopping in the cornrow next to mine.

Was I happy to have company out there? Not hardly.

Lordy, but I was glad when she announced she was gonna have to go in and start getting dinner ready. I like to killed myself trying to keep up with her and even so couldn't quite manage it, and wasn't that an embarrassment! Once she was out of sight I could slow down a little again. Long enough anyways to wipe some of the sweat out of my eyes and peer out onto the desert. If I'd had a horse and a gun . . .

Except no, dammit, I wouldn't've either. I'd come here to have harsh words with some fellas and get my five thousand back. Nobody was holding me here against my will; I was free to walk away anytime the notion struck.

But walking away wasn't what I came here to do and there was no pretending otherwise.

So I kept whacking—slower now—and was more than just a little grateful when I heard the angle iron clang. There's never been a carillon sound as pretty as that old piece of scrap metal sounded to me right then.

I dropped my hoe right smack where it was—figured if she asked I could just say it was to mark the place where I'd left off, even though that was about as obvious as a skunk walking on snow—and headed first for the outhouse and then for the washbasin and soap bucket at the side of the house. I was plenty ready for lunch.

Got around a whole lot of it too once the praying was done and I could leap on in.

No meat again, but that didn't surprise me this time. Just more of the same. Rice and biscuits and lots of milk gravy.

Breakfast had been different, though. Pancakes and cactus jam along with some biscuits and gravy.

It was surely a good thing Mrs. Kaufman could cook biscuits as good as she done.

"I'll be going to town this afternoon, Mr. Johnson," she said as she gathered up the dirty dishes and deposited them in a bucket of soapy water. "I'm sure you will be all right here by yourself."

"Yes, ma'am."

"Finish with the corn if you can. If you have any time to spare, you might carry water to the vegetable garden. You'll see where my irrigation ditches start. Just keep pouring water in." She smiled. "I don't think there's much chance you could overwater them."

"Uh . . . no, ma'am, I suppose there isn't at that." Could be she'd noticed me dogging it once she left the cornfield earlier. "Is there anything else?"

"No, Mr. Johnson." The smile got bigger. "I'll be sure to return before the cows need milking."

"Yes, ma'am." I went back to the corn and the weeds and the hoe and the ground that was hard as aged hickory. A little while later I heard the creaking of some wheels and looked to see what was causing it.

Got a surprise I did, too.

Now, it is a really strange thing when I think about it, but it hadn't struck me right off. The thing was, there were no horses on the farm. No riding horse, no draft horse, and not so much as a plow mule.

There was a wagon, all right. I'd seen it parked beside the barn and hadn't paid any particular mind because there's wagons everywhere you look. But here there wasn't any horse around to pull the dang wagon.

So it was a good bit of a surprise to me when I looked toward the house and saw Mrs. Kaufman heading off toward town. On foot. With a wheelbarrow.

It was a big barrow with an iron tire on the wheel and rags wrapped around the handles to make it a little easier to lift and shove. She had two of those milk-can things riding way forward in the bed of the wheelbarrow, placed so their weight would act as a balance and once she got the handles up and balanced all she'd have to worry about was pushing and not lifting.

Even so, it wasn't going to be an easy trip into town for her. The place was a good five miles off. Call it nearly two hours walking if a body didn't have a wheelbarrow to contend with. And that much back again. Mrs. Kaufman was going to be gone the rest of the day and perhaps then some.

I chopped corn just as dutiful as you please until she was out of sight, then dropped my hoe again and went over to the house to get a drink of water.

While I was in there—I will admit it—I nosied around just a little bit. You know. Just in case.

Either the late Mr. Kaufman hadn't been a hunting man or the Widow Kaufman was one of those women who disapprove of firearms and killing little creatures or something—she hadn't yet put any meat on the stove, had she— but for whatever reason, there wasn't a gun in the house.

Not that I'd counted on knowing where I could lay my hands on one. But it never hurts to find out these things.

I made sure everything was exactly the way I'd found it, then went back outside and set in to chopping weeds like a madman to make up for the time I'd wasted.

25

"WHO ARE YOU?"

"I know who you are. You're Mr. Johnson. Mama told me all about you." Which I hoped was an exaggeration. All? I shudder to think of it. Still, her comment did answer my question. Sort of. Mama would presumably be Mrs. Kaufman. And this kid would be . . . ?

"D'you have a name?"

"Of course I have a name. Everybody has a name."

"Not everybody," I told her. "I knew a man once who didn't have a name. We would have called him No-Name except he wouldn't let us. Said that would become his name, and he didn't want a name. So we didn't call him anything at all after that."

"What happened to him?"

I shrugged. "I don't know. Tried to ask somebody about him once, but I didn't know who to ask after and so I never found out."

"You're funning me," she accused.

"Yes, I am. Now, are you going to tell me your name or not?"

"I am Leodyce Evelyn Kaufman. But you can call me Evie."

I squinted a little and looked her up and down. "And

you're—what?—ten years old? Eleven maybe?"

"I am ten. Will be next month anyhow. How old are you, Mr. Johnson?"

"Three days older'n dirt," I told her.

Evie Kaufman was a skinny, blond little thing if perhaps a mite tall for her age. That was just my impression, though, and a lot of that based on her mama being so tall. After all, what the heck do I know about little girls. She had freckles and blue eyes—the genuine article; I still hadn't figured out what color eyes her mother had—and a scabbed-over scratch beside her left eye where something had gotten her pretty good.

"Do you know Mr. Donald Payne, Mr. Johnson?"

"No, ma'am, I do not."

"Mr. Payne is Susan's daddy. Susan is my best friend. Susan is ten already. She had a party. That's where I've been. Staying with Susan, I mean. After the party. It was last weekend. Everybody in Willow Creek came, and I got to stay over seeing as Susan is my best friend."

Which was the first I'd heard the name of the town that lay up-valley.

"Mr. Payne owns the bank there."

"I see." A regular little fount of knowledge, young Evie was. And her best friend's daddy owned the bank. Terrific. I expect that was what I was presumed to've robbed in order to get the five thousand four hundred dollars they hanged me for. Now all I needed was for blabbermouth here to go telling her best friend about the man who was chopping weeds down at the Kaufman farm.

The best I could do, I supposed, was to hope they wouldn't make a connection even if something was mentioned.

Come to think of it, why would they? Far as those seven were concerned, the robber was hanged and long since dead and the money recovered. I should be safe enough here.

And Evie could sure be a source of information.

"Here." The child shoved a piece of flour sacking at me.

"Mama sent me to bring you a fresh towel. You're to wash up for supper now."

"Thanks."

She turned and started back toward the front of the house but after a couple steps stopped and turned around again. "Is it true that you don't know how to milk a cow? Really?" She sounded like that was about the oddest, most strange thing she'd ever heard.

"It's true," I assured her. "But I could rope one for you." I grinned. "If I had a horse and a rope, that is."

"You're a cowboy? Wow! I didn't know that bums could be cowboys too."

She sounded impressed. But . . . *bum?* I've thought myself to be a fair number of things in the past, but bum hadn't ever been one of them. Until now, that is.

"Oh, yes indeed," I said. "Lots of cowboys turn into bums. But not very many bums turn into cowboys."

"That doesn't make sense."

"It isn't supposed to."

"Oh. All right, then." She grinned, a positively impish expression, and went skipping off to do whatever it is that little girls do.

I turned to the washbasin. It was near full dark, and after a day of whacking weeds I'd built up a hunger that was going to take a spell to do away with.

26

"ARE YOU GROWING a beard?" It was the kid who asked. She was as full of questions as she was of information, I was discovering. We were sitting at the table after supper—which consisted, unsurprisingly enough, of rice and milk gravy followed by biscuits with jam for dessert—having a cup of hot milk with honey in it. Mrs. Kaufman was busy washing dishes.

"Yes, I am," I said, deciding it pretty much at the same time as the words came out of my mouth. After all, though, I had neither a razor to shave myself nor the wherewithal to buy a shave in town. Dang whiskers were itching something terrible just under my chin, though. Which was probably why Evie asked about it, seeing as I kept digging and scratching there.

"It makes you look like a gruff old bear," she said.

"There are worse things than that," I told her.

"Name one."

"That sounds to me like a challenge."

"Evie!" her mother cautioned without looking up from her washing.

"I wasn't complaining," I said. "I don't mind a question or two."

Mrs. Kaufman didn't say anything, so Evie repeated her question.

"Worse than a gruff old bear?" I mused. I could think of an awful lot of things, actually. But I figured it was best to confine my list to something a kid would understand. "How 'bout a billy-goat gruff," I suggested. "That's worse than a gruff old bear."

"No," she said, taking it quite seriously. "I don't think so. A billy-goat gruff would only butt you in the tummy and make you fall down. A bear would eat you all up, and then you'd be dead. Like my daddy. He's dead, you know."

"Yes," I said. "I know." I got the idea that was something she'd been wanting to work into a conversation and that most any excuse would have satisfied her. "Your mama told me that."

That seemed somehow to satisfy her. Just so I knew.

"You can start drying now, Evie. Finish your milk and bring your cup now."

"Yes, Mama."

I polished off the last of mine too—it was good with the honey mixed in—and Evie carried my empty cup to the wash bucket along with hers.

"When we are finished here, Mr. Johnson, I'll want you to take your clothes off."

"Ma'am?" I knew there was no point in getting excited by that information. Not with Evie there.

"Those things you are wearing are filthy, Mr. Johnson. And if you don't mind me saying so, they smell bad too. I'll want you to fill a tub . . . I'm heating bathwater for you now . . . so you can scrub yourself too. I will lay out some of my husband's things. I think you are close enough in size that they won't be too bad a fit. While you are bathing and changing, Evie and I will go out to the shed and see if we can't do something to make a more comfortable bed for you."

"Yes, ma'am." I gathered she was assuming that I intended to stay awhile. And I guess that indeed I did.

After all, with different clothes and a beard, it wouldn't be too awfully long before it would be safe for me to go into Willow Creek and poke around without having to worry overmuch about being recognized as a dead man come back to life.

✤ 27 ✤

IT WAS JUST as well that I didn't have a mirror. This would've been embarrassing.

I looked, I was sure, like a . . . farmer.

The late Mr. Kaufman's clothes fit me okay. A little long in the leg and the sleeves and a trifle loose in the waist but otherwise okay.

No, the problem wasn't with the fit. It was in the selection.

My clean clothes—and it's true that they smelled and felt an awful lot better than the things I'd been wearing for this past and almighty difficult week—consisted of fresh cotton drawers, home-knit socks, a blue shirt of some rough and durable fabric, and—get this—bib overalls. Bib dang *overalls*! I'd never had on a pair of bib overalls in my life. Until now.

It was humiliating, that's what it was. And yet the bib overalls weren't even the worst of it.

My farmer outfit was capped—literally—with a . . . a cap. A cloth cap. A flat, floppy, stupid-looking cloth cap. Humiliating? Lord, I reckon.

I, who'd been wearing nothing but John B. Stetson for about as long as I can remember or anyway as long as I wanted to remember, was reduced to draping a stupid cloth cap over my noggin.

I could just imagine the comments I'd get when I walked into Willow Creek looking like that.

Didn't want to call attention to myself in town? Huh! Anybody show up on public streets looking as dumb as I did in those clothes and folks would surely come from miles around just to point and stare.

And maybe the oddest thing of it all was that neither Mrs. Kaufman nor Evie acted like they thought the least thing wrong with this crazy getup.

The truth is that I felt kinda like a kid dressed up for a costume party on All Hallows' Eve or some such.

The only thing I had left on that I walked in with was the boots. And those miserable damn things hadn't even been mine. They'd belonged to that posse-riding, quick-to-hang son of a bitch who'd stolen mine.

It was a low state I'd come to, I'm telling you true. A sad, sad state of affairs indeed, and it was only the direst of necessity that kept me from turning around and marching right straight back into the desert I'd so recent come out of.

The direst of need, that is, and five thousand dollars.

Damn those men anyway.

✛ 28 ✛

"YOU NEEDN'T REACH for that hoe, Mr. Johnson. We will be going to town today." She smiled. "You are welcome to come with us if you please."

"Ma'am?" I finished pouring the new milk into one of the big cans and rapped the lid with the heel of my hand to make sure it was tight enough that air and dirt and bugs couldn't get in.

"It is Sunday, Mr. Johnson. We'll be going in for services." The smile returned. "Won't you come with us?"

I rubbed my chin. The beard was coming along nicely. And in my farmer clothes, well, nobody I'd ever known my whole life long would figure out it was me. "I hadn't kept track of the days, I guess." Which was the truth. Sunday wasn't anything that'd ever much mattered to me except as a day off from work and that only sometimes.

"Will you come?" she pressed.

"To town, sure. I dunno about . . . you know."

"As you wish, Mr. Johnson. You know you are welcome to join us."

"Yes, ma'am, thank you."

"We will take the milk in today too, of course. I take it in Sundays and Wednesdays. More often if the weather is especially hot." So that'd been a Wednesday when she took the milk to town before and came back with the little girl in tow. I hadn't known that either, what with the days sort of running together when there wasn't need of them.

"Yes, ma'am." She didn't have a proper springhouse with running water but made do by keeping the big milk cans stored in a tub of water that was freshened with cool water from the well every evening after the heat of the day was past.

"There are clean clothes for you inside. Evie will have them ready for you by now. You'll have time to change before we leave."

I'd been hoping for something presentable, but these clothes were the exact same as the first set, though fresh-washed and smelling nice. I changed into them and Evie collected the others, ready for Monday wash day.

Mrs. Kaufman had on a dress that was as shapeless as her everyday ones but not quite so faded, and she'd added a bonnet with some genuinely ugly fake flowers pinned onto the side of it as her dress-up deal. Personally, I thought she looked better in the turban rig she generally wore. Or just with her hair let down loose like she kept it in the evenings. But then what the heck do I know about women. Or girls.

Evie's Sunday outfit was a cut-down and made-over version of her mother's. She had a little round-top straw hat with a brim and ribbons. Cute. If she'd had better-looking shoes, she'd've looked properly spiffy. As it was, all she had were her old brogans, the sort of thing you can buy cheap out of a catalog, and they were old and a couple sizes too big for her. I kinda thought they must have belonged to someone else at some point, but I sure didn't want to ask about that and embarrass the kid.

I loaded the milk cans—two of them just like Mrs. Kaufman had taken in before—into the wheelbarrow, and we were ready for the five-mile walk into Willow Creek.

Dang woman was stronger than I'd realized. When I picked up on the handles of that wheelbarrow I found that

it was a load to manage even after I got the balance right.
And she'd pushed it by herself the whole way on Wednesday. And come to think of it, every Sunday and Wednesday
before that since her man died. She was one tough female,
by damn.

"Are you ready, Mr. Johnson?"

"You just lead the way, ma'am. I'll be right behind."

"Evie. Come along, dear."

And so we went, Mrs. Kaufman and Evie striding right
along down the dirt track and me huffing and puffing with
the wheelbarrow behind them.

WILLOW CREEK WAS bigger than I'd thought. There was a grove of mature cottonwoods strung out along the creek—which I assumed was also called Willow—but not a single willow in sight. Go figure.

The outskirts had houses and boardinghouses, and the central part had one street lined on both sides with stores and saloons and the like. It was ordinary enough really except for being bigger than I'd expected. Big enough to have its own bank, two hardware stores, and a pair of churches set side by side and well apart from the fringes of the business district where all the saloons were. I knew that because I was following Mrs. Kaufman and Evie and they led me clean through town and almost out the other end to where the churches were before we got to the house—I'd expected a store, but this wasn't one—where the milk was delivered.

I carried the heavy milk cans inside a springhouse, the real thing with cold water diverted out of the creek or maybe an artesian well someplace nearby and piped through, and left them there. Mrs. Kaufman didn't go rousting the owner out for her milk money right away like I would've done. Or even go tell him the milk was there. But then I suppose this was a long-standing arrangement and both parties knew what to expect of the other.

"You can leave the wheelbarrow over there, Mr. Johnson." She glanced up the street toward the churches, one of them Protestant and the other Roman judging from their outsides, then turned back to me and said, "Will you join us?"

"No, ma'am, but I thank you for the offer."

"As you wish." She reached into a pocket on her dress and brought out a faded but once rather fine little silk coin purse that she opened and dipped into. Then without comment or explanation she handed me a dime.

It didn't seem much. But then when you figure what ten cents could mean to a widow with a growing kid to raise and a hardscrabble farm to run, well, that dime was a lot bigger than it looked. My thanks were as sincere as I knew how to make them, and I hope she knew that.

"Meet us back here at two o'clock, Mr. Johnson. And do be prompt if you please."

"Yes, ma'am."

"There is a clock in the front window of the bank. You can judge by that."

"Yes, ma'am." I'd paid some attention to the bank when we came by it and had noticed the clock put there where the public could see. What was that banker's name again? Evie's best friend's father? Payne, that was it. The daughter was Susan. I couldn't recall the father's name right off. Not that it mattered.

"Yes, well . . ." She hesitated for a moment more and I thought maybe she was going to press me to go along with them to church, but she didn't. She bobbed her head in a "that's that" manner, then turned and marched off toward the churches with Evie alongside.

Me, I left the wheelbarrow beside the springhouse where the milk was kept and turned back toward town.

It was a Sunday, but far from all of Willow Creek's residents were inside those churches. It hadn't escaped my attention that back in town all those saloons were open and doing a lively trade, judging from the yelps and the laughing and the biting, yeasty smell of beer coming out of the open doorways.

✣ 30 ✣

IT SEEMED CRAZY but my stupid looking farmer clothes
didn't draw a single odd look from the crowd in
Mackey's Dust Cutter saloon. Believe me, I was prepared
to be laughed right back out of the place, so I was paying
close attention. No one so much as noticed.

But then once I was inside the place I could see why.
Nearly everybody in there was dressed pretty much the
same as I was. Or close enough that the differences didn't
matter. I mean, not so many were wearing bib overalls. But
apart from that, well, there wasn't much to choose from.
Most of the men enjoying their day off wore rough clothes,
shoes instead of boots, and either cloth caps like the one I
was cursed with for the time being or silly little narrow
brim city hats, derbies, and bowlers and the like.

Seemed strange out here in the middle of nowhere, but
this dry and dusty little town was citified through and
through. I would've expected this to be ranch country. And
mighty big-range ranch country at that, seeing as how it
would take so awfully much land to support a single cow.

But no, there were plenty of folks living here and so far
the only cattle I'd seen were dairy cows and most of the
few horses around were heavy-bodied pulling stock.

That was definately a mine of some kind that I'd seen

over on the north rim not too far west of the town itself, and I expect that explained it. The population was here to work in and otherwise support that mine, and if there weren't ranches or other forms of empty-country businesses around, the whole shebang would collapse and die if that mine were to play out of ore—whatever kinda ore it was.

Which, once I got to thinking on it, more or less explained why those sons of bitches in the posse were so hostile toward me when they thought I'd robbed their payroll.

Anything that threatened the mine would threaten everything and everyone here. And if the mine was operating on a slim margin, well, I'd think the loss of five thousand dollars—excuse me, five thousand four hundred—I'd think that sort of loss could really hurt a business if it was just barely making out.

Now mind, I was doing this pondering and observing inside the Dust Cutter while at the same time making sure I wasn't standing out from the crowd.

I'd come in and headed for the far end of the bar and stood there, where I was mostly hidden behind two enormous blond Scandahoovians. I dunno where these boys came from, but either one of them could have stood in harness in place of a Percheron dray horse. Maybe they spoke some English but not to each other, so I couldn't understand a word they were saying. Being downwind from them, so to speak, I could tell they'd taken pains to clean up for their day in town. They both smelled of soap and bay rum, and their clothes were fresh-laundered.

They gave me room enough to squeeze in between them and the sidewall, and when the barkeep came near I laid my dime down and nodded.

He took the dime away and returned a moment later with a beer and a nickel change. "You're new," he said.

"Uh-huh."

"Looking for work?"

"Could be." I reached for the beer and buried my nose

in the head. The beer was cool and biting and clean in my throat, and out on the desert I'd've killed for a drink of it. It tasted almost that good to me still, now that I was remembering anew what those possemen had put me through, damn them.

"Man can most always find something over at the C 'n C," the barman said, trying to be friendly and helpful. Which I truly did appreciate. I had no quarrel with him.

"C and C?" I asked.

He inclined his head toward the north, in the general direction of that north wall where the mine was located. "Willow Creek Chromium and Coal Company." He paused. "Limited."

"Limited?"

"It's owned by a bunch of Englishmen. We say 'incorporated.' They say 'limited.' Damned if I'd know why."

I looked around. "These guys are English?"

"Not hardly. The Englishers that own the company don't mingle with us peasants. For that matter, I don't think any of 'em show up in this country more than once every year or two."

"Absentee ownership," I said.

"About as absent as you can get."

"Is that bad?" I asked.

He shrugged.

"Coal and . . . crow something?" I said. "I never heard of coal mixing in with anything else."

"Chromium is the other one. And they aren't coming outta the same hole. There's a good vein of coal at Anderson Butte, about eight miles north of here. They take the coal out there and fetch it down here to fire the mill. Then they reduce the ore to take the chromium out and ship that off to sell. Neither one would be commercially useful without the other, see. Because of the distances. We're so far off from the railroads that it wouldn't pay to haul the coal or the raw ore either one. But they can use the coal to process the ore, see, and just ship chromium. It works out fine. And the company is pretty much always needing men. If you're interested, that is."

"Thanks for the advice and the explanation, friend."

He smiled. "Always willing to put a newcomer in my debt. That way he'll be sure and come spend his money in my place." The smile extended into a grin and he reached across the bar to offer his hand. "I'm Paul Mackey. This is my place."

"It's a pleasure, Mr. Mackey." I shook the man's hand.

"Paul," he corrected. And gave me an expectant look.

For a moment there I like to panicked. I couldn't for the life of me remember right off what name I'd told Mrs. Kaufman. Then I was able to relax. "Wesley Johnson," I said. "Just call me Wes."

"Pleased t' meet you, Wes."

"Likewise, Paul."

"Care for another beer, Wes? This one's on the house." He laughed. "It's just another sneaky way for me to make sure you'll want to come back to my Dust Cutter."

"Since you put it that way, Paul, yes, I'd surely enjoy another."

He picked up my mug, which had gotten emptied somewhere along the way, and carried it off to the taps.

Yessir, there is nothing like a friendly saloon when it comes to learning things.

31

I SPENT MY Sunday time off standing there at the bar of the Dust Cutter, nursing my three beers—one on the house and two that I had money to pay for—slow and gentle so as to stretch the time out as far as I could.

All I got out of it, though, was the beer. Not a single one of the men who'd been in that posse showed themselves inside Paul Mackey's place.

Believe me, I had every one of those men's faces memorized too. I would have recognized them even if they'd been in a condition to hide from their own mothers.

I didn't count it time wasted, though. Just time spent. There were other places in Willow Creek to be looked into—I never for one minute considered looking for sons of bitches like those inside the churches, of course—and each and every one of those possibilities would be investigated before I counted this deal done.

At the rate I was going so far, though, it was going to take a while.

I drank my three beers slow enough for my Scandinavian neighbors to down seven apiece. And after that the sons o' guns didn't so much as wobble when they waved good-bye to Mackey and left the place. Seven beers would've put a buzz in my noggin and that well-remembered numbness in my cheeks and nose, but the intake didn't seem to faze them in the least.

For my part, I could feel it just a little bit after only three, but I kinda attribute that to it being so long since I'd had anything to drink. Three, four weeks? Something like that, what with the travel I'd done intentionally and then the travel afoot that I'd had no choice about.

Once my third mug was emptied long enough to get dry on the bottom, I figured it would be impolite to stand there gawking at the clientele any further. Conspicuous too, maybe, and if there was anything I purely did not want to do, it would be to draw attention to myself.

Beard, farmer clothes, and all, I did not want to risk one of those possemen spotting me and wondering what a dead man was doing walking around on the streets hereabouts.

A man would have to be a first-class believer in ghosts to let that slide by.

So I caught Mackey's eye and mouthed a silent "thank you," then went back outside.

The sun was high overhead and I judged it wasn't yet close to the two o'clock time Mrs. Kaufman said I should meet them, but just to make sure about that, I walked down the street to the bank.

MINERS AND MERCHANTS CHARTER BANK, the sign read. Gilt leaf on the window glass added, C. DONALD PAYNE, PRESIDENT. Donald. Sure. That was the name of Evie's best friend's father.

According to the clock in the window, it was 11:56. I had two hours to kill and no money to help me do it.

No money. Dammit. Now that I realized it was lunchtime I got to thinking about lunch. Naturally. There'd been a free lunch spread laid out at the other end of the bar back in Mackey's, but I hadn't been hungry then. And hadn't especially wanted to go out amongst the patrons either. Now, just a couple minutes later and knowing it was time to eat, I was feeling so hungry I'd've happily gone looking for a rattlesnake or jaybird to eat again.

One thing I'd learned—and had reinforced right thoroughly over the past week or so—was that activity will help to ward off hunger pangs.

So, having no money to buy food with but strong legs and good feet to walk with, I took off to treat myself to a tour around the town of Willow Creek.

I hiked along as if I knew where I was going, with the idea that someone who knows where he's going has a right to be going there and isn't likely to be noticed very much. I went first along the creek bank, which was lined with cabins and small houses that looked older than most of the other buildings in town, then around behind the churches and looped back down the southern outskirts, just kinda looking things over and getting an idea of the lay of the place.

Down toward the southeast end of both the town and the grove that it lay in I saw a long, low-roofed sod building that looked older than the dirt it was built with.

The place had no sign hung outside, but then it didn't need one. There were four sturdy hitch rails nearby and every one of them close to full with saddle horses. And I noticed that there wasn't a single wagon, buggy, or light carriage parked anywhere in the vicinity.

I stood in the shade, just kind of leaning up against the trunk of a tired old tree. While I was watching three men came out and turned toward the furthest bunch of tied horses.

I couldn't get a look at them as they were facing away from me. But there was one thing I spotted first thing.

That sonuvabitch on the right side was wearing *my* damned Stetson hat.

I guess I wouldn't've been much surprised if steam started coming out of my ears about then, but I couldn't see to check on that my own self and there wasn't anybody around to ask.

Damn them!

32

B Y THE TIME Mrs. Kaufman and Evie showed up, I was mighty full of the fidgets. I'd been idling around beside the creek there at the milk buyer's house until I thought I'd bust from impatience. But I didn't calculate that I had much choice about it.

I couldn't just disappear, not without risking losing my meal ticket at the Kaufman farm, and so I had to talk to Mrs. Kaufman before I took off trying to follow those three riders.

It was clear from the get-go that I couldn't've kept up with the men, not even if I was a runner like one of those short-pants college boys that run long-distance races for the fun of it. I mean, aside from the fact that a man on foot isn't going to keep pace with a horse, I had to worry too to keep out of sight.

When those three rode away from that hog ranch, I knew good and well that the best thing I could do was to get a look at what direction they were going and then follow them long afterward.

They headed off to the west, striking along the fringes of the town and continuing on past the churches. I was able to see that much before they disappeared from my view and were gone.

Keeping track of them that far put me already on that end of town, so I just hunkered down and stayed there.

After what seemed like half a damn day but probably wasn't much over an hour Mrs. Kaufman and the kid showed up. They looked . . . nice. Fresh-faced and smiling and full of good cheer.

I got up off my hind end and touched the itty-bitty brim of my cap and said, "If you don't mind, ma'am, I'm gonna stay in town awhile longer. But don't you fret about the wheelbarrow. I'll bring it back this evening when I come."

"I can take it with me, Mr. Johnson. It's all right."

"No, ma'am, I wouldn't feel right about that. I'll do it."

She gave me a sad sort of look and said, "Mr. Johnson, you don't have to be polite. I know what you are wanting to do this afternoon."

"Ma'am?" It startled me. I mean . . . she didn't. Couldn't. I knew that. But her saying that kinda startled me anyway.

"You want to go over to the C and C, don't you? You're going to apply for work there, aren't you? Not that I can blame you. They pay three dollars a day underground, two and a half on top." She smiled. "It hardly compares to ten cents a week, does it?"

"Ma'am, I said I'd be back, and so I will. I said I'll bring the barrow, and so I expect to do."

"If you say so, Mr. Johnson."

"I do, ma'am."

"Then please be so good as to load the empty cans in and bring them with you." She showed me where to find them and which to take—there were upward of a dozen spanking-clean cans in a lean-to beside the springhouse—and gave me another doubting look before she finally told me, "In that case, Mr. Johnson, please excuse us. We will . . . see you later, yes?"

"Yes, ma'am. Count on it."

I could tell she was anything but convinced, but she didn't argue the point any further. Evie gave me a little wave and walked backward for a dozen steps before her mama whispered something to her and she turned about and walked proper and little-lady-like on down the street.

I watched them on their way for a minute or so and then made my way past a whole herd of folks who were streaming past after services just like the Kaufmans had done. The good folk of Willow Creek were headed back into their town while I was sneaking out of it and quickly out of sight along the bank of the creek.

My question now was whether I could find the place where those men had got to. And then see could I do something about it—about them—once I found them again.

✢ 33 ✢

IT WASN'T EXACTLY difficult to follow the man with my hat. Him and the two others took the road west from town, and there was only one. That was a good thing since the further away from town that I got, the less brush there was along the creek banks and the less cover to conceal me. About a mile upstream from the town of Willow Creek the water lost all pretense for its name as the greenery disappeared altogether, so there were only bare, stony flats on either side of the creek and the banks sloping upward until there was soil enough to support some grass.

Once I lost the protection of the foliage, I felt pretty naked out there with no gun, not even my slungshot along for defense. Not that it would've done me any real good. But I might have felt somewhat better about things if I'd had some sort of weapon to hand. It was my judgment however—not, thank goodness, my experience—that chunking a rock at somebody would not be much protection against a .45 slug, so maybe it was just as well that I wasn't carrying the sling anyhow. This way I had no choice but to avoid trouble.

I followed the rutted and very frequently traveled road for maybe a mile and a half to an improved ford leading over onto the north side of the creek.

You could see where the triple tracks of another, very old road split off at that point to continue up the south side of the creek. I couldn't tell where that road went, but it wasn't used very much if at all these days. There wasn't a fresh hoofprint in that middle track nor any sharp-edged tire tracks on the outer ones.

Up to that point the road was cut deep and wide from the passage of large wheels and big horses but with only a whisper of a center track to show that light, single-horse rigs ever used it at all. This offshoot road looked like it'd only been used by one-horse outfits and not an awful lot of them in recent years.

Somebody had gone to a lot of trouble and expense to pave the ford where the main road crossed over the creek and headed toward the C and C mine. Slabs of sandstone had been cut and laid in place across this wide, shallow spot so wagons could safely cross without having to worry about what was underfoot.

Obviously this ford was well used. And important to somebody.

I stood there for a bit looking off toward the north, to the buildings of the C and C, then accepted the inevitable and kicked off the scraps of leather that used to serve that highway-robber son of a bitch for boots. Bad as they were I didn't want to get them wet and make them even worse. As it was, they were so bad that I almost wished the late Mr. Kaufman had had some spare shoes to hand down when he went to his reward. I would almost have been willing to be seen in public wearing brogans just to get out of having to wear these boots. Or what was left of them after I'd cut my sling pocket off them. Miserable damn things! Miserable damn robbers that made me to wear them!

I rolled my pant legs up a few laps and waded barefoot across the ford, determined to find some satisfaction, damn 'em all.

34

I FOUND SOMETHING, all right. It was trouble.

The heavy-traveled road headed straight as a stick toward the mine buildings that spilled down the north face of the valley wall, but about a quarter mile off from the creek another much lighter-traveled wagon track veered off from the main road and headed west.

Like the one south of the creek, this one showed three beaten lines indicating use by light rigs. The difference was that this triple track was used regular. From what I could judge, though—and mind, I'm no great shakes at tracking anything or anyone—the most of its use these days looked to be riders on horseback and not wagons of any sort or size.

Now, between the fact that it didn't seem likely to me that any fellows wearing boots and big hats should be headed off toward a danged mine and that the SOB with my Stetson was a horsebacker, well, it seemed sensible to me to leave off the main road and turn west.

I was about three-quarters of a mile along and still hadn't caught sight of whatever was up there toward the head of the valley when I heard the beat of hooves behind me.

Truth is, I'd been so intent on looking in front of me, in the direction where I thought that posseman would be, that

I hadn't paid any particular mind to what might be happening behind my back.

That was a mistake.

I looked back and saw two men coming.

And one of those bastards was riding my horse.

My own damned horse. And me without a gun.

I would've hidden except for two pretty good reasons otherwise. One was that these fellows were only eighty or a hundred yards back· of me and had to've seen me long before I ever heard them back there. The other reason was that even if I had spotted them, there wasn't anyplace to hide.

This flat where I was walking was bare of everything except scattered rocks and sere, browning bunchgrasses. This side of the creek, I'd found, was mostly dry, as the grass showed good and well. The subsurface spread of water was confined mostly along the south side of the creek, so over on this side it was far from being desert, but the grasses were more a high plains growth than the lush, bottomland grass I'd got used to seeing on the south side.

The only reason that interested me right off was that over here there just wasn't a damn thing to hunker down and hide behind.

Oh, if I'd been smart enough to pay attention and sharp-eyed enough to see those riders before they spotted me, I could've managed to hide myself. Probably.

It's a funny thing, but most often a person can hide himself almost in plain sight.

A man who has no reason to be especially vigilant will generally be looking fairly far off from the spot where he happens to be at any given moment. And he'll give the most of his attention to what's in front of him.

What I mean to say is, a man riding a horse will look down the road he's traveling and for the most part he'll see whatever is, oh, anything from fifty yards ahead to a quarter mile. Then every once in a while he'll kinda sweep his gaze side to side and look away off. Say to a half mile or farther.

But he won't generally examine the ground right close by on either side of his path. He won't really concentrate on it, that is.

So I didn't have much choice but to stop and stand there and wait for those two riders to come up to me.

Dammit.

35

"Y OU'RE ON THE wrong road, bub." It was the guy riding my horse who spoke, and there wasn't anything friendly in his voice. He kinda growled the words out.

The good news was that even though he was on my horse, he was not one of the men who'd been in that posse. He hadn't been part of the hanging party, damn them all to hell.

The other one looked sort of familiar to me, but he hadn't been with them either. I couldn't really place this man. Maybe I'd passed him on the street back in town or else he'd been one of the customers in Mackey's saloon. It could even be that he simply reminded me of somebody else. Not that it mattered anyhow.

"They might be hiring at the mine," this one said, "but not on Sundays. Nobody in the office on Sundays."

"This is Sunday, is it?"

The one on my horse—but not my saddle, I noticed— said, "There's nothing at the ranch for the likes of you, bub." He gave me a look like I was a bug on the wall that ought to be swatted. Because of my farmer clothes, of course. Men on horseback generally have nothing but contempt for men afoot, and men who wear boots and big hats will always look down on some damned fool who shows up in public wearing bib overalls. Truth was, of course, I would've thought the same as them had our situations been reversed. "You best turn around and go back."

"I'm hungry, mister. You wouldn't turn a man away hungry, would you?"

"Bub, we already did that. Now turn around and get the hell outta here before we teach you some manners."

"But you wouldn't—" I didn't have time to finish the rest of it. The SOB jabbed with his spurs, and my own damned horse bolted forward and slammed me hard with his nigh shoulder.

I hadn't been expecting that, them coming at me without a by-your-leave or a par'n-me, and I got knocked flat. I landed on a rock that hit hard in the small of my back, and the air went whooshing right out of me. I felt the stab of pain in that area, then the back of my head smacked down just as hard. From the inside it sounded like a melon being thumped, and I commenced to feel all numb and tingly.

The second one tried to ride me over and then the first one right behind him, and for a few seconds there all I could see was hoofs and dust and horses's bellies. Those sons of miserable bitches were reining their horses 'round and around and trying to get them to stomp on me, but of course they wouldn't. The horses, I mean. If there is anything a horse hates, it is to step onto something that is soft or uncertain as to the footing, and generally speaking, a horse will turn itself purely inside out before it will step on a man or a calf or something like that on the ground. An animal pretty much has to be trained special for the job if you want it to stomp on anything short of a snake. Most horses and pretty much all mules will stomp the hell out of a snake if they have the chance.

Anyway, these two damned riders were trying to get their mounts to stomp on me, and me, I was laying there trying to force myself to be still and not give in to a panicky impulse to try and roll out from under all this commotion. That was because while the horses wouldn't want to step on me, if I got to wallowing around too much I might cause one of them to take a misstep and trample me by mistake. So I tried, with limited success, to force myself to lay still while those two fellows were whooping and whistling and lashing their animals into tight, whirling turns.

Bastards!

I managed to roll facedown and drew my knees up high and the moment I thought I had a few seconds in the clear I came up off the ground hard and fast.

Those sneaky Apaches didn't have too bad an idea of how to go about things, and I took a page outta their book. When I made my leap I came up with a rock about the size of an apple in my hand, and I came up swinging it.

Jumped high and grabbed the one I'd been thinking of as "bub," for his use of it when he talked to me. I latched hold hard on his left wrist and pulled, yanking him halfway out of the saddle, while with my right arm I took a wide swing.

The rock in my fist connected with the back of his head, and I'd like to think it was only the fact that he had a good hat on that saved him from having his skull busted clean open.

As it was, he went loose in the saddle, and I pulled him the rest of the way down to my level and commenced thumping and kicking just as hard and fast as I knew how.

I was getting him pretty good if I do say so. But it didn't last near long enough.

His pal jumped his horse into my back and knocked me loose of Bub and then came down onto me like he was trying to wrestle down a steer.

I was still pretty groggy from that whack on the back of the head when I was knocked down the first time, and the guy had me from behind.

Which is all by way of an excuse for admitting that this other SOB was waling the bejabbers out of me and beating up on me awful bad.

I was lucky, I suppose, in that the guy left off beating me when he saw that his pal was hurt. Mister Two gave me a few parting kicks and then concentrated on getting

Bub onto his horse—*my* horse, dammit—and on down the road in the direction of this ranch where they didn't welcome anyone in bib overalls, not even hungry travelers so dressed.

I lay in the dirt there and watched them ride off, and it occurred to me that somewhere up in that direction there were more just like these ones and they might well be coming back to finish the lesson Mister Two had started.

It took me a few minutes to get my legs back under me and truth to tell I was afraid for a while there that I'd be crawling away from that spot instead of walking, but after a time I was able to keep myself upright and propelled in more or less the direction I wanted.

Didn't seem a very good idea to stay on that road where I'd be easy seen, so I headed straight south until I got back to the creek, then lay down at the edge of the water so's I could drink and rest and get my faculties back to . . . well, to as good as I ever have them, not that I make any fancy claims about that sort of thing.

I laid there until it was near dark and was glad that I did because off in the distance I could hear an occasional shout and now and then the passage of horses.

I don't know for sure that there was a bunch of riders from that ranch out looking for me. But I don't know that they weren't either and didn't want to take any chances about it.

Once it was dark enough that I thought it safe, I stood up—it was easier to do by then anyway—and headed back toward town.

I still had an awful long way to walk and much of that time with a wheelbarrow and some milk cans. What was waiting for me at that end of the trip would be a whole lot better than what I would've found at that ranch, though, had I gotten that far.

I've heard it said that folks should be thankful for small things.

Right then I reckon that I was.

✦ 36 ✦

I'VE NO IDEA how late it was before I got back to the Kaufman farm. Truth is I don't entirely remember doing it. But that's where I woke up the next morning. I woke to the sight of Mrs. Kaufman kneeling beside me where I was laying just outside the barn.

The wheelbarrow was laying toppled over on its side next to me, and I could see one of the two milk cans that would've been in it when I started out walking from town.

Everything seemed sort of blurry. Not my vision, I mean, but my thoughts. Everything was fuzzy and jumbled together, like for instance, I knew what I was looking at but it didn't make sense to me. I saw Mrs. Kaufman's mouth working and I heard that she was making sounds, but I didn't have the least idea what those sounds were supposed to mean.

That was . . . scary.

Either because I was so scared by all this or because I was awake now or, hell, I dunno why exactly, but I chose that particular moment to puke.

The lucky part was that I hadn't had anything to eat in an awful long time, the unlucky that there was still some fluids in me. I don't know if I splashed any onto the lady. I hope not.

I tried to sit up, but she held me down flat and turned and shouted out something real loud, and pretty soon the little girl—Evie, although just at that moment I couldn't remember her name—she came running out of the house.

I could see then that it was coming dawn. There was a glowing, violet sort of light out to one side and a biting chill in the predawn air. Maybe that's why I was shivering so hard.

"Help me, honey. We need to get him inside."

"In the shed, Mama?"

"Yes, I . . . no. No, I think we'll need to keep an eye on him closer than that for a while. We'll take him into the house. Help me now. Get over on that side, dear."

The child's voice was disapproving. "He's drunk isn't he, Mama?"

"No, honey. I thought so too at first, but there's no smell of whiskey on him. And see how he's been bruised there? I think he must have fallen down somewhere."

"Or someone beat him up, huh?"

"I don't think anyone would do that, dear. He probably fell down or . . . something."

"He really isn't drunk?"

"No, dear. Now help me. Lift. Hard. That's the girl. Again. Now . . . pull, honey. Pull real hard."

I had a vague sensation of movement and then what little light there was faded away. When the light got strong again it was from another direction and was a clearer, yellow light. A lamp, I decided later. At the time all I heard were the sounds, and those had no meaning.

I thought . . . hell, I dunno what I thought. I wanted to say stuff and I wanted to ask stuff and I wanted . . . I wanted to shut my damn eyes and let the world go away for a little while longer.

So that is what I did. I just let go and let everything slip off to someplace else where I wouldn't have to be bothered trying to sort it all out.

✦ 37 ✦

I T WAS THE strangest damn thing. I could see and hear
things just fine. And after a time I could even figure out
what it was that I was seeing and hearing. More or less.
But it was like I was . . . I don't know how to put this
proper—it was like I wasn't really there. Like I wasn't
really a part of it all. I had the same sort of . . . detachment
I guess you could call it . . . as if I was just reading about
somebody else, and it was this somebody else that was
doing the seeing and the hearing.

Does that make sense? It didn't to me, exactly. But that
is as close as I can come to explaining it, I think. It was
like I was standing off someplace else and watching while
somebody else lay on that bed hurting and dizzy and confused.

Did I mention hurting? Lordy, I reckon. My head, it was.
Thumping and pounding and throbbing to beat the band. I
could feel every time my heart beat. The rush of blood that
my pulse caused hurt so bad I could hear it as well as feel
it. It was about all I could do to lay still and not jump up
and try to run away from the hurting.

Not that I could've done that if I'd wanted to. I was dizzy
just laying still. I can't imagine how it would've been if
I'd tried to sit up. And stand on my own hind legs? Not

until this hollow, dizzy, detached feeling went away, thank you. Try and stand up like this and I'd just fall down and hurt myself all over again. That was pretty plain to me even at the time.

Mrs. Kaufman and Evie stretched me out onto Mrs. Kaufman's own bed and pulled my split-out and run-down old boots off and covered me over with a quilt.

The quilt was clean and pretty, and I felt bad about her putting it on me because I was so dirty and smelly my own self. But when I tried to tell her that, the only thing that came out of my mouth was some babbling, bubbly sort of noises that hadn't ought to do with proper words.

I knew what it was that I wanted to say.

I just couldn't make my tongue perform the acrobatics that was needed to form those thoughts into words.

Funny as hell, isn't it?

Well let me tell you something. It isn't funny worth a damn when you try and do something you've been doing your whole life long without ever once having to think about it and then of a sudden you can't manage it no more.

It scared me when I realized that.

It scared me bad, and I was awful pleased to just let go again so's I could sleep and not have to face up to being like this.

My last thought was a hope—I've never been a praying man, but I think I came pretty damn close to it right then—that I wouldn't stay this way permanent.

Lordy, not that, please.

✢ 38 ✢

I HEARD A sound, which I now think that I must've made myself, about half from the hurting and the other half a matter of being scared because I was coming more or less awake and couldn't see anything. I think that just for a few seconds there I kinda thought that I'd gone blind in addition to all this other stuff and so I sorta groaned or let out a croak and that is what I heard that woke me the rest of the way up.

I remember forcing my eyes real wide open and not seeing a glimmer of anything.

A few seconds more and I could make things out. More or less. The place was almost but not quite totally dark. I seemed to still be lying on Mrs. Kaufman's bed with the quilt pulled high to my chin.

It pleased me to know that I could make these things out without having to fumble for the meaning of what I saw and sensed.

Overhead I could hear the creak of boards shifting and then a moment later saw a pale shape descending from above. I was well enough in touch with things to know that this wasn't some spirit floating about but just Mrs. Kaufman coming down from the loft in her nightdress. With me in her bed, I guess she'd gone up there to sleep with Evie.

She must've heard the noises I made when I woke and now she was coming down to check on me.

I didn't feel up to raising my head but didn't have to in order to watch while she came down the narrow ladder, barefoot, and went over to the stove.

The hint of light in the room became just a wee bit stronger when she opened the door to the little patent range, and it became considerably brighter yet when she poked into the coals with a hay stem or wisp of straw. She used that to light an oil lamp on the table, then carried the lamp over so she could hold it high and see to check on me.

I smiled and tried to nod a hello. Nodding was a mistake. That set the drums inside my head to pounding again. But the smile was heartfelt, believe me.

"You're awake," she said.

"Yes, ma'am." My tongue worked just fine without me having to think about trying to guide it, and I knew both what she'd said to me and what I wanted to say back to her. That was a powerful lot of improvement over the way I'd been before.

"Are you hungry?"

I hadn't much thought about that. But now she said it, my belly felt so empty I thought it had gone all hollow. "Yes, ma'am."

"You should be. You've been passed out cold for almost three days."

Three days? I would've guessed something in the hours, not the days. Lordy!

"I've been . . ." I didn't know how to put all of the things I wanted to say to her. "A trouble to you," I said.

At least she had sense enough to not deny the truth of that. She smiled and said, "Let me get something to put in your stomach."

Oh, that did sound like a fine idea. Chicken broth. That would be the best thing, of course. When somebody's been bad hurt or taken down sick, there is no finer remedy than chicken broth. I thought about that and my mouth got to watering something awful. I swallowed back the spit and that bottomed out in my stomach and made me feel sour and queasy, but I hadn't any control over it.

Mrs. Kaufman went over to the stove and pushed some twists of dry hay in to start a flame, then added small pieces of dried cow dung and then bigger ones until she had a good fire going. She fiddled and fussed over there for a bit and soon enough came over to the side of the bed. She dragged a chair near and sat on it and gave me a looking over for a moment.

"We're going to have to prop you up, Mr. Johnson. Do you think you can stand that?"

"Yes, ma'am."

She put an arm under my shoulders so that she was supporting the back of my head and lifted with that arm while she used the other to shove a pillow behind me.

It was silly but I felt like she lifted me up too high, and I got more than a little dizzy. I think I would've thrown up again except there wasn't anything there to heave.

Something else that I couldn't help but notice when the quilt slipped down from under my chin was that my chest was naked. The last I knew I'd been fully clothed. Now . . . I didn't know what else I wasn't wearing or how I'd gotten this way. Wasn't right for me to be like this, not around a child and a decent woman. But I was and I'd had no say in it. It did make me uncomfortable, though.

Mrs. Kaufman plumped the pillow and considered for a moment, then got another to tuck in behind me so that I was raised up off the flat of her bed a little.

"Is that all right?"

I nodded. I was afraid for a moment if I opened my mouth it would be more than words that came out. But nothing happened right off, so I nodded again.

"Good." She turned away and got a tin cup that she carried back to the bedside, where she sat and held the cup to my lips.

Turned out to be calico tea, not chicken broth. About

half and half milk and hot water and some sweetener mixed in.

I knew enough about Mrs. Kaufman's situation by then to realize what a sacrifice she was making for me by giving me expensive sugar mixed into the calico tea.

This was a woman who hadn't hardly anything, and I wasn't but a stranger to her. Yet she was giving me the best that she had. Little though it was, she was giving it to me.

The warmth of it reached my belly and spread through me, and I smiled but can't now remember if I thanked her after I finished half a cup or so of the sweet mixture. I can't remember because without me hardly knowing the difference between waking and sleeping, I slipped off again to a quiet, healing place.

✠ 39 ✠

I WOKE UP looking at a slender, balding man wearing a handsomely tailored suit and a gold watch chain and fob that must've cost as much as a handmade D. Hirt saddle. With tooling on the skirts and everything. The saddle, I mean. Watch chains don't have skirts.

It occurred to me that maybe I was still pretty far from being back to normal because this man was saying something to me and there I was thinking about a custom saddle that I'd seen—what?—six years before.

"Excuse me?"

The man blinked and stopped talking. Mrs. Kaufman came up behind him. In a regular dress and not her nightdress. That prompted me to notice that it was daytime now, which it surely hadn't been the last I'd been capable of noticing anything.

"I'm sorry," I said. "I guess I looked like I was awake just then, but I'm still kinda hazy about things. Am I s'posed to know you, sir?"

"Mr. Johnson, this is Mr. Payne."

The name sounded about halfway familiar but I couldn't figure out just how or why.

"Mr. Payne is a friend of the family," she added by way

of an explanation that did not, in fact, explain very much. At least not to me it didn't.

"My daughter and Evie are best friends," Payne put in. Which jogged my memory some. Payne was the banker. Same bank that had a clock in the window. I could remember that now. But not his daughter's name. The one who'd had a birthday recently. My head hurt.

"I drove down to see if everything was all right here after Brady told me about the milk can."

"Milk can? What milk can? And who's Brady?"

"You don't remember?" Mrs. Kaufman asked. "I told you all about it yesterday evening."

"Ma'am, I don't remember yesterday evening, never mind what mighta been said then. I'm sorry."

She looked worried then and came over to bend low and peer close into my eyes for a bit. "You look better now," she announced.

"Yes, ma'am. I feel better now. There was, uh, something about a milk can? And somebody named Brady?"

"Charles Brady is our neighbor on the place next up the road toward town. He found the milk can you lost."

It was my turn to blink. "I thought I brought them back with me."

"You did manage to bring the wheelbarrow home and one of the milk cans, although God only knows how you managed that in your condition. The other can was lying in the road. Mr. Brady saw it there and set it aside for me two days ago."

"And when I heard I naturally assumed something was amiss," Payne said. "The people hereabouts are fond of Mrs. Kaufman, you know. We all are. No disrespect intended, Mr. Johnson, but I am very much relieved to find that it is not she who's laid up."

"None taken," I told him.

"I am pleased to know she has a hired man now to help her around the place," Payne said. "Are you from around here, Mr. Johnson?" He made the question sound just as casual as casual could be.

"No," I said. End of comment. If Payne wanted to go fishing he could walk down to the creek, but I wasn't biting. My bell might've been rung but I wasn't so fuzzy-headed that he could get me to blabbering about myself that easy.

"Are you hungry, Mr. Johnson?" Mrs. Kaufman asked.

"Yes, ma'am."

"Do you feel up to having something solid today?"

"Yes, ma'am, I surely do."

"I'll make you something to eat. Excuse me, gentlemen." She turned away. Payne watched her go, then pulled a chair close and sat beside me. Mrs. Kaufman got busy mixing a batter, and Payne smiled at me.

"I'm glad you are feeling better now, Mr. Johnson."

"Thanks." Not that he meant it. The man didn't know me from Adam's off ox.

"Will you be staying on here?" he asked. "After you are on your feet again, I mean?"

"For a while, I reckon."

"You'll not be looking for, shall we say, better-paying opportunities?" When I didn't answer he added, "I could give you a recommendation if you want to hire on with the mine. I happen to know they're needing teamsters to handle the coal wagons."

"Is there some reason you're wanting me off this place, Mr. Payne?" I asked him point blank.

"No, I . . . not at all, Mr. Johnson. Certainly not."

I smiled at the man. "Mr. Payne, you're setting there wondering why I'd stay here an' work for my keep when I could go hire out for a regular wage."

"I didn't mean—"

"Of course you did. You just didn't want me to think so. But you did."

"All right, perhaps so. Now, will you answer the questions? The ones I've asked, I mean, and the ones implied?"

"No, sir, I don't expect that I will." I grinned and threw in a, "No disrespect intended."

"I wonder if it might be best for me to arrange proper nursing care for you in town, Mr. Johnson. Your recovery might be more . . . comfortable . . . there."

"Mr. Payne, I am just naturally one stubborn and contrary son of a buck. But I will tell you one thing, and I expect it gets to the bottom of those questions that you haven't quite asked out loud. My reasons for wanting to stay here and help Mrs. Kaufman on her farm aren't anything that could bring hurt to her nor to Evie."

I wish I'd been right about that. God knows I believed it at the time.

Payne sat there for a few moments looking at me. Then, apparently satisfied at least for the moment, he nodded and stood up. "If you will excuse me, Mr. Johnson?"

"Pleasure t' meet you, Mr. Payne." And it sorta had been at that. For sure it brought me fully awake and back in touch with what all was going on around me.

✛ 40 ✛

AFTER ABOUT TWO days of being awake and rational and laying in bed while Mrs. Kaufman and Evie waited on me, it finally got through my thick head that there'd been a few changes since I first came here.

Before, the staple food was biscuits and milk gravy. Good stuff, that. And cheap.

Now the food Mrs. Kaufman was cooking and serving was even cheaper. There was still plenty of milk and milk gravy to be had, but she wasn't baking those fine biscuits anymore. Now she was making corn dodgers. Hoecakes, I've also heard them called. Biscuit-sized lumps of corn-meal dough baked in a Dutch oven like the biscuits are but more coarse and in truth not quite so tasty as wheat-flour biscuits.

But then cornmeal is an awful lot cheaper than the wheat flour.

My presence, being here and eating my way through what little they had, was costing that woman and little girl too much.

I promised myself to make it up to them once I got some money in my pockets.

Not my five thousand, though. I'd had plenty of time to think while laying in that bed, and I realized now that there just wasn't any five thousand to get back again.

Whoever stole that payroll was no doubt out of this country long since, and my five thousand would've been distributed among God knows how many employees out at that mine. Looking at the thing dispassionately, I was just gonna have to accept the fact that what I'd had was gone now and the best I could hope for would be to take whatever I could from those sons of bitches who'd hanged and robbed me.

But that, I vowed, I was damn sure gonna do.

Just as quick as I could get on my feet again.

Easier thought than done, though.

Once I got to thinking about that, of course, I couldn't be satisfied without sitting up on the side of the bed—which I could manage with only a little strain and struggle—and giving it a whirl.

Bad idea.

I was no sooner standing up than my head felt like it was spinning fast as a kid's tin top. I got dizzy and lost my balance. Tried to turn around so as to fall face first onto the bed—ever notice that practically nobody ever falls down backward? It's true; if you're gonna topple you'll just naturally do it forward without something or somebody pushing you back—and only halfway made the turn before my knees buckled and I went down. Hard.

I hit the side rail of the bed hard enough that it's a wonder neither me nor it broke.

I think I hollered, but there was no one in the place to hear me, as both Mrs. Johnson and Evie were outside working or whatever.

I was still lying there on the floor, hurting something awful and woozy but mostly awake, an hour or so later when Evie came in and found me like that. She let out a cry and ran back outside to fetch her mama.

Seemed I wasn't doing too good as a patient to their nursing.

But I was mending. Damn right I was mending. And I had time enough to think long and hard about what I could do once I was able to get around proper again.

GRAY. MRS. KAUFMAN'S eyes were gray. That was one of the things I'd studied out while I was laying there in bed like a useless lump. Those pale, pale eyes were most definitely gray. Except for sometimes in the evening twilight or again in the false dawn, when they looked blue. But they were really gray. I was almost sure of it.

Truth is, I was paying way too much attention to Mrs. Kaufman. Thinking things about her that I oughtn't.

Which is not to say that she wasn't a handsome woman, for she was. Tall and lean and more than a bit windburnt and leathery from the hard, outside work all the time. But all in all not a bad-looking woman. And as it had been quite a spell since I'd been with any woman, well, I suppose it was only natural that I'd be interested.

Even so, nature or not, it wasn't right nor proper for me to be thinking of her like that.

Mrs. Kaufman was a decent woman. The genuine article too.

God knows I'd had little enough to do with any decent women in the past and for sure I'd never spent any serious amount of time around one before now. Never stayed under the same roof with an actual decent woman nor got to know the way they could be in the evenings, cleaning the house

after supper and teaching Evie stuff and singing tunes that
sounded sort of half-familiar, so that I thought I should
know the words to them but didn't.

It was . . . nice. That's the only way to put it. It felt nice
to lay there on the bed like a mouse in the corner, quiet so
they acted like there wasn't a stranger among them.

Seeing Mrs. Kaufman and her little girl together in the
evenings, listening to them and watching them in their
home, it made me feel good and never mind the hurts that
still needed healing. This was a good feeling of a kind that
had nothing to do with was there pain or wasn't there.

The truth is that I liked it and kind of wished . . . aw, it
didn't matter what I wished. Wishing won't buy a man a
whiskey nor so much as the smell of one. Best I should
keep in mind who I was and what I'd come here for, because decent ladies like Mrs. Kaufman weren't for the likes
of me and I knew that as good as anybody.

It wouldn't take a man with a gold watch and expensive
fob to tell me. I already knew.

"Mr. Johnson."

"Ma'am."

The skin at the corners of her eyes crinkled and squin-
ched tight when she smiled. Funny thing, but I liked that.
"I didn't realize you're awake."

"I just now woke up." I hadn't, but for some reason
didn't want to admit to the truth.

"Evie, dear, why don't you get Mr. Johnson a cup of hot
milk, please."

The little girl nodded and went to the stove without fussing or complaining that she'd been given a chore.

They seemed to've run out of sweetening the day before
or so because Mrs. Kaufman had given up on the calico
tea—which I liked—and was just heating milk so it would
be more like a proper beverage. Milk and sometimes I'd
even seen her heat plain water for herself and drink that
without anything at all in it for flavor. That was serious

saving if she was even trying to stretch the milk so she'd be able to sell more in town.

Damn but I was a drain on them. I hated it, but there wasn't anything I could do different.

Soon, though. Real soon, I thought.

✢ 42 ✢

"LIE DOWN, MR. Johnson. You aren't strong enough to be out and around quite yet."

"I'm feeling fine. Really."

"That may be true." I thought I could hear more than a little skepticism in her voice, but at least she was polite about it. "But really, Mr. Johnson, you aren't ready to be out doing things."

"I won't do much. Just a little," I insisted.

"Have it your way, then."

"Thank you." It struck me as I was on my way out the door that I'd just thanked her for letting me go do some work. And if that wasn't strange—me, who'd spent most of my lifetime trying to avoid work—well, it was weird, that's what it was, weird.

But I did want to try and help around here for a change instead of laying about drinking their milk and eating their food.

So out the door I went.

The sunshine hit me over the shoulders like a hard lick with a singletree, and it occurred to me that maybe, just maybe, Mrs. Kaufman had a point. I practically went to staggering from the impact of the sunlight alone.

Still, I can be one stubborn so-and-so. And I'd said I was gonna do some weeding in the corn patch.

First I went out and let the cows in from their little pasture and put them inside the barn. By now we'd all accepted the fact that on my best day I wasn't going to be a milker. That squeeze-and-grab stuff . . . I just couldn't get a handle on it, no pun intended. Evie could milk a cow almost slick as her mama could. I just made them cows mad whenever I tried, and then Mrs. Kaufman or Evie had trouble convincing the stupid things to let their milk down after I got done riling them. So I'd given up trying. Wasn't anything wrong with me letting them into the barn, though, and saving that much effort for somebody else.

I distributed a little grass hay into the bunkers and fetched one of the big, wide-bladed hoes from the corner of the barn nearest the front doors. Mrs. Kaufman was just coming out to the barn as I was leaving it, so I stood aside to let her by.

Seeing her there in the daylight . . . it was funny how I hadn't particularly noticed right off what a good-looking woman she was.

She must've seen something in my glance because she raised an eyebrow, but I only shook my head to tell her it wasn't anything—and it *wasn't* either, dammit, and couldn't ever be—and went on out to the corn patch with the hoe in hand.

Mrs. Kaufman, I'm afraid, was more right than I'd expected her to be. I hadn't hoed a dozen feet of row before my head was all swimmy and my balance most somewhere past the horizon. I was tottery and weak and began running a cold sweat even though the morning sun was plenty hot.

Trying to work . . . it was a mistake.

I finally smartened up enough to accept the truth of it and went back to the house. It tells you how weak I still was that I had to lean on the hoe like it was a cane or a staff or something just to keep from falling over sidewards, and even at that I was close to not making it. Had to stop twice to catch my breath and gather strength again before I could get all the way around to the front of the house.

I knew better than to try and put the hoe away in the barn, so I left it standing propped against the wall and went inside to darn near collapse onto a stool.

Evie wanted to run get her mama, but I told her no, there wasn't need for that. I did accept a cup of hot milk from the child, though. And shook so bad I like to spilled it getting it to my mouth. I felt a little better once the warmth spread through my stomach. The cold sweat left off and I quit trembling so bad.

Soon, though. I'd be just fine soon, I told myself. Not today maybe. But soon.

✦ 43 ✦

NEXT TIME I got to feeling strong and sassy I didn't try it out in the dang corn patch. Next time I thought I was up to walking around, I decided I'd try and do some good. And quit eating the Kaufmans out of house and home while I was about it.

"If you don't mind, ma'am, I'm gonna go off for a couple days until I feel up to being a proper help around the place."

"But you can't, Mr. Johnson. You aren't up to that yet. Besides, where will you go? What will you do? You don't have anything to eat and I haven't any money to give you. What will you do, Mr. Johnson?"

Damned if she didn't sound like she really and truly cared about all that too. I was . . . I just wasn't used to anyone giving much of a damn what became of me. The concern in her voice and even more so the worried look in her pale, pale gray eyes, they touched me someplace where I wasn't used to letting people go.

I'd been thinking about it, though, and had some thoughts on what to do now.

The boys who'd stolen my money and hanged me by the neck until they *thought* I was dead, they were still out there, each and every one of them. I'd come to realize that I wasn't like to get my money back. But that didn't mean I wasn't still plenty upset with them. I figured to get something back. Down-and-dirty satisfaction if not the cold cash.

And those boys who'd hanged me, they seemed to be nesting, so to speak, at that ranch or whatever it was out toward the head of the valley.

They'd spotted me coming the first time I tried to get out there.

That wouldn't happen a second time.

"Won't you at least let me pack you a dinner? I could bake a little corn bread," Mrs. Kaufman offered.

"You've done too much already," I told her. And I meant it. She was a really good woman. I'd heard about those before, of course. It pleased me to've found one now for maybe the first time ever.

"But what will you do? Where will you go?"

I smiled at her. "I'll be fine, ma'am. I been taking care of myself a good long time now. I'll handle it."

"You'll come back?" she asked.

I hesitated. It might could be, considering what I had in mind, that my best course would be to do what needed doing and then get the hell out of this valley. Far and fast away from it.

But, well, I owed Mrs. Kaufman and Evie. That was sort of a new thing to me too. I owed them. Imagine that. And it was the sort of debt that involved a whole lot more than just money. They'd taken me in when I was hurt and they'd treated me more than just decent. They'd been genuinely good to me. That wasn't the sort of thing I could easy forget, and I wanted to do something back for them. Fill their larder with good things to eat. Do a heap of the work that needed doing around the place. I dunno. I just wanted now to do for them. It hardly mattered what all I wound up doing. Just so they'd know how much I appreciated their kindness.

"I'll be back," I told her. "That's a promise."

I don't make promises easy and don't regard them light.

Not that she would know this. But I sure did.

I fetched that dumb-looking cloth cap down off the peg where it'd been hanging the past two weeks or more, touched the brim of it, and let myself out into the low, slanting light of late afternoon.

If Mrs. Kaufman thought this an odd time of day to be setting out for a walk, she didn't say anything, and I was glad for that. I'd've hated to have to go and lie to her now.

IT WAS FULL dark by the time I got to town but just barely so. I could still see a tinge of orange low in the sky to the west to show where the sun went down over that end of the valley. The stores along the main street had all closed down for the night and by now most decent folk should be sitting down to their suppers while the saloons and hog ranches should be just getting about their sort of business.

I found a small eatery tucked into the middle of a block of businesses between a greengrocer and a freight agent. The place looked to be good. It was swarming with folks, and the smells reaching the street were enough to set a man's mouth to watering even if he'd just finished a fine meal. Personally, I hadn't had a fine meal, not one with any meat included, in a powerful long time. Was my mouth watering? I reckon and then some.

Empty pockets and all, I sauntered inside.

The proprietor was a man whose hair had all drooled down off the top of his head and reemerged out his ears. He needed a shave and the apron he was wearing was none too clean, but he seemed a pleasant enough sort. Soon as he saw me he came to me, snaking his way between the tables, and said, "There's an open chair at that table, mister.

And we don't cook to order. Supper is two bits. Ham hocks and cabbage tonight, all you can eat."

It sounded mighty fine, and if I'd had the two bits I would have spent it and gladly. As it was, I apologized and said, "I've already et myself, neighbor, but I was hoping to find Jerry Tucker in here. Have you seen him?"

"Tucker, you say? I don't believe I know him," the eatery man allowed.

Now as for myself, I really did know Jerry Tucker. Or used to anyway. We were maybe ten, eleven years old at the time. Still, I made something of a show of looking around the room and—wonder of wonders—not finding old Jerry.

"Not here," I said. Then, as if it just occurred to me, I rubbed my belly and said, "Neighbor, I think I'm getting a touch o' the runs. D'you have an outhouse around back?"

"Sure thing. You can go through that way." He pointed toward the back of the place, through what I was sure was the kitchen. And which was the exact reason why I'd picked a place in the middle of the block and not one that sat on a street corner or next to an alley.

"Thanks." I bobbed my head and went back there.

The cook was a fat woman with arms like a lumberjack and her hair plastered to her head from the sweat. Her stoves—she had two of them—were radiating heat enough I wouldn't have thought she would need to put anything into the ovens. Just set a bowl of dough on the big table in the center of the room and it would surely bake without being moved from there. She was busy messing with something inside a deep, black enamel pot and didn't so much as look around at me when I passed through.

Which I did. Through the kitchen and out the back door. By the time I got outside again, though, I had a big old ham bone in my fist and a couple light and puffy dinner rolls, yeast rolls that'd been buttered on top before they were baked, in the other hand.

I went around behind the outhouse to where the air was

fresh and gnawed that bone until it was polished. There was an awful lot of good meat left on it when I got it, but hardly anything'd been wasted by the time I was done. Lordy, but that did taste fine. Meat. I'd been missing it.

The rolls were good too, and I worked on those in between bites of the ham. Plenty good meal, I thought.

It hadn't taken me so awfully long to get around that ham and soft bread. When I was done I tossed the bone to a couple scrawny-looking dogs that'd come creeping near. Which might've been a mistake. There was two dogs and only one bone, which resulted in some snarling and growling. But I figured they would work that out without my help, so I went back inside the café.

"Mind if I wash up?" I asked.

The fat woman grunted and pointed and went back to her stove. I'd already spotted the washstand and basin next to the back door. I washed the ham grease off my fingers and freshened up with a splash of water on my face and then dried off on a towel that was spanking clean and smelled of sunshine.

"Thanks."

The cook didn't say anything nor pay me the least bit of attention.

By the time I thanked the waiter out in the café, who I supposed would be the fat lady's husband, I had another pair of those good rolls in my left-hand pants pocket and a couple raw potatoes in my right-side pocket.

Breakfast was assured.

I stood outside enjoying the night air for a minute or two, then paused to do some thinking. Did I want to head out to that ranch place right off or not?

Not, I decided. There was something else I wanted to do first, no longer being the innocent and trusting soul that I used to be.

I headed off down the street in search of a nicely rowdy saloon. But not the Dust Cutter. I liked Paul Mackey, who ran that one, and wouldn't have wanted to do anything that might reflect badly on him or his place, after all.

✤ 45 ✤

THE CHEAP AND dirty place out on the edge of town where I'd seen that guy from the hanging posse was ideal for what I needed. It was set off away from other businesses a little distance, and it had an outhouse of its own out back. And outhouses were a fairly prominent part of my plans for the evening.

With my belly full and a good idea of how I wanted the rest of the evening to go, I found a comfortable spot behind a clump of tall weeds growing close to the outhouse.

There was no moon to see by, but the sky was clear and the stars bright. That helped some. And there was a spill of lamplight through some windows set high under the eaves of the hog ranch.

Off to my left there was a low-roofed line of cribs, five of them, each cubbyhole about six feet across the front and maybe eight, ten feet deep. They were attached all in a row, and a couple small lamps were affixed to the front wall of the building and left burning turned low, to guide the girls and the patrons to their, um, pursuits.

I had no interest in the men and women who were moving in and out of the cribs, though. All I wanted from them was that they be intent on what they were doing and paid no mind to the world around them. That didn't seem too much to ask, and I thought I could probably expect to get it, everything considered.

Not that there was so very much traffic to and from the cribs for me to worry about. I was hazy on what time of the month this was but gathered that it wasn't particularly close to payday around here or the working girls would've been busier than that.

That worked out just fine, though, as there was no one else wandering around when my pigeon came flapping and staggering out of the saloon on a mission to make room in his bladder for the introduction of more beer.

The guy was perfect. Still early in the evening and already this jehu was snockered. He was weaving and wheezing and damn near tripped over himself twice on his way along the hard-beaten path to the outhouse.

Very nice, I thought.

I stood close beside the outhouse wall, sure that I couldn't be seen in the deep shadow there and equally sure that this poor damn drunk wouldn't have noticed me if it'd been high noon and I was tooting a tin whistle. He was pretty much out of things.

Which was just what I wanted.

While he was fumbling with the door, I stepped around behind him and whacked him over the head with a flat chunk of rock I'd had the foresight to collect when I first got there. I hit him hard, but not so hard that he ought to be seriously hurt. I didn't want that.

The guy collapsed like a poleaxed shoat. His knees went out from under him and he dropped without a whimper.

I caught him under the arms and dragged him around behind the outhouse and laid him down—gently as I could manage—ready for picking.

I did have one small regret. I should've waited until he'd been inside the outhouse and was on his way back. Because while I could've waited, he couldn't. And while normally I wouldn't much care about that, this time it annoyed me. Dang drunk's pants pockets were sopping wet when I went through them.

✢ 46 ✢

I'D GONE PROBABLY a half mile, grinning and walking on air, when I realized that I'd forgotten something that could give me away. Dammit! So back I went, not running but picking them up and putting them down right smartly in my newly acquired footwear. Shoes in this case instead of the boots that I much preferred, but they fit just fine and felt perfectly wonderful after those broken-down boot pieces I'd been wearing for all this time.

I hurried around back of the outhouse and discovered that my drunk hadn't been hurt very bad because he'd already come around and managed to walk, crawl, or hobble elsewhere.

That was fine by me. I didn't have any beef with the man. It was just that I needed some of his stuff if I intended to accomplish anything here.

Lucky for me, those twice cast-off old boots were still lying where I'd left them. It had occurred to me while I was walking in my new shoes that those old boots could sure be recognized if the wrong folks spotted them, and I didn't want anyone tipped to the fact that the innocent man they'd hanged was still alive and now lurking around in the shadows. No sir, I didn't want to take that chance.

I picked up the boots I'd so casually tossed aside and

took them into the outhouse. They made a dull, squishy splash when they hit bottom, and I figured I was pretty safe from having them discovered now.

I went ahead and made use of the facility while it was handy, then once again set out into the night to see just who I could find and what I might could learn.

Figured it should be safe to follow that same road off to the west end of the valley now, seeing as it was fully dark, and even if some of the riders came along again, it would be easy for me to hide from them.

Felt considerably safer too because now I had a pistol in my pocket.

The poor drunk that provided it wasn't much of a judge of firearms. The dinky little gun wasn't but a breaktop revolver in one of the smaller, rimfire calibers.

It was much too dark for me to be able to read the impressions on the frame and top of the barrel, but I was betting that come daylight I would find that I was carrying a Smith & Wesson in .32 caliber. Those aren't powerful worth a damn, and they only hold five pipsqueak cartridges. But five .32s beat hell out of a slungshot any day of the week, and I was glad to have it.

Besides, a small bullet does the damage just fine if you're careful of your placement. And one well aimed shot of any size will beat hell out of a cannonball that misses its mark, and most anything will beat a fast noise. So all in all, I was satisfied with the little Smith.

I'd stuffed it into a back pocket, my front one being already occupied by the potatoes that I'd swiped back at the café.

And I even had some money in the same pocket with those spuds. I had no idea yet how much was there because there wasn't light enough for me to decide were the coins silver or gold. But whatever, whether those were silver quarter dollars or the same size twenty-dollar double eagles, I had some jingle to part with now if I needed to buy food or ammunition or something. And it's always better to buy something nice and open and legal rather than hide out in the dark and whack a man so you can steal from him.

So yeah, I was in a mighty high humor as I marched out along the road leading west from Willow Creek. I had food in my belly, money and a gun, and more food in my pockets.

Now all I needed was to find those sons of bitches who'd hung me. I fingered my shirt collar and rubbed at my neck some as I walked, the remembering of it bringing back some of the pain and burn their rope caused me. Damn them.

I WAS LUCKY. They didn't keep dogs. There is nothing like the snarling of a dog in the night to put the fear into someone who isn't supposed to be there and nothing like the barking howls of a dog to bring somebody out with a shotgun in his hands. I was glad these people didn't want the nuisance of dogs on the place for I surely didn't want that either.

As it was, I found the place easy. Just found the path and followed my nose and there it was about two miles west of the larger road that went out to the mine on the north bluff.

It didn't seem all that much of a place. There was a house and some pens like you'd expect at a ranch headquarters and a long building that I took to be a bunkhouse. Those were normal enough, but I was surprised by some open-front low-roofed sheds erected to one side and all the more so by the absolutely huge stacks of hay that'd been built nearby. In the dark I wasn't sure just how many haystacks there were, but I could plainly see half a dozen and had the idea there might be even more beyond the range of my vision. They'd been built with heavy teams and angle stackers, and each one of them stood so tall they looked like small mountains.

I remembered that I hadn't seen all that much in the way of cattle when I was coming into the valley.

But then somebody'd said the mine used an awful lot of freight wagons to haul coal in and processed ore out, and freight wagons require horses and lots of them.

I crept around a bit out of sheer curiosity and found that sure enough, most of the horses in the holding pens were heavy cobs with thick bodies and big feet. They wouldn't be much as saddlers but would be just the thing for hauling freight.

The low, open-front structures turned out to be equipment sheds with mowers and rakes parked there under cover and some wagons in various states of disrepair. One small building held a wheelwright's forge and vises and another was given over to woodworking tools. I found a couple stoutly built carts too, of the sort a man might use when he wants to teach a young horse to pull.

Apparently, what this place was was a sort of repair depot for the mining company's wagons, and a training and, for all I knew, a breeding ranch for the horses to pull those wagons.

That made sense.

Curiosity satisfied on that account, I went around behind the house and kinda slithered up behind it.

It was easy. No dogs, remember. I hardly had to worry about it because there wasn't any guard posted. These boys were evil-tempered, but they weren't up to anything that they were trying to hide.

I walked soft to keep from being heard but otherwise was in plain sight had anyone been watching. Went right up to a glassed window and stood there sort of off to one side so I could peep through and see what-all they were up to.

The place looked like it maybe once was used as a regular house but now it was more of a barracks than a home. There were no beds in here—those would be over in the bunkhouse, I suspected—just easy chairs and tables and a big old cooking stove against the back wall where I was.

There were about a dozen hands inside, yakking and playing cards for the most part. One fellow was playing a mouth organ. Another was braiding horsehair; I couldn't tell yet what the end result would turn out to be, but he was concentrating on doing a good and careful job of it, whatever it was. A couple fellows were arguing loud enough that I could almost but not quite catch some of the words, but through a closed window and with other noise going on in there, the sounds were indistinct and all kind of muddied together.

That was all right. I couldn't hear them but they sure weren't likely to hear me stomping around outside either.

Every once in a while one of them would get up and leave—maybe on his way to the bunkhouse to turn in, maybe headed for town, I didn't know—or another would wander in.

It was impossible to tell for sure without going out to the bunkhouse and counting beds, but I'd've bet there were eighteen, twenty, maybe more than that number of hands working out of this place.

That seemed a lot, but then I didn't know how many wagons and teams the mining company would be running.

Didn't care about that either, of course.

But there was something that I did damn sure care about.

And that was that inside this house I could see four of the seven sons of bitches that'd come and hanged me.

Four of them. Right here at one time.

The little Smith & Wesson like to burned a brand onto my hip as I stood there looking in at those bastards and feeling the weight of the gun in my pocket.

Four of them, and not a one of them knowing that I was still alive.

I guess I began to tremble just a little about then.

✣ 48 ✣

I MIGHT'VE MADE a mess of things right then and jumped in too soon. For sure I was tempted to it. But I was saved when there was some more traffic in and out. Two fellows who'd been playing cards dropped out of their game and left and about the same time that one man came in.

It was the leader of that posse. The tall, lean SOB they'd called Cap.

Him I wanted more than all the rest of them put together. Well, him and that miserable sonuvabitch that kicked me. Dave, that one's name was.

Dave and Cap I wanted the most of all. And of the two of them, it was the leader of that pack of curs that I wanted more. I held him responsible more than any of the rest of them. He's the one could have stopped it. Instead he egged it all on.

And he was the one I wanted to pay me for the trouble I'd been put to.

If I had to let the rest of them go—and that was a strong possibility once word got around that I hadn't died at the end of that rope after all—I might be willing to do that just so long as I could get full satisfaction out of Cap in there.

I thought about that. Just how much satisfaction there would or could be.

The easy way out would be to stand right out here, take careful aim, and empty the little Smith & Wesson through the window into the man. Hell, he was only—what?—fifteen feet away from me right this minute?

Fifteen feet away but on the other side of a pane of glass too. Which meant the first bullet would likely stray after busting through the glass. That dropped my possibilities to the four measly bullets remaining. Out of a gun that I'd never fired—for that matter only assumed *would* fire—and which had a completely unknown point of aim. And to top that off, the man would be a moving target as soon as that first, sure-to-fail shot busted the window. All he'd have to do would be to drop to the floor and he would be hidden behind the tables that filled the middle of the room.

No, standing out here and trying to shoot him down from ambush didn't seem all that good an idea. Not, you understand, that I had any scruples about shooting the son of a bitch from hiding. I'd've done that in a heartbeat and never thought about it after.

It's just that I didn't think it would work out for certain sure. And this was something I damn well intended to be certain sure about.

Better to wait for my chance. And to keep hidden until then. There was no sense in showing myself and getting beat up again or worse than that. And a change of clothes and now fully grown beard weren't necessarily going to protect me from being recognized if I was caught and hauled before that bastard Cap a second time.

Better to take that chance, I thought, by keeping an eye on these boys until they all went off to bed.

My plan, such as it was, would be to watch and see where they all went. Then, when everything was quiet and they were all asleep, I'd just kinda slip inside and find Cap while he was snoring. Poke the business end of the Smith & Wesson into his ear and find out just how much damage one of those wee-bitty .32 slugs can do inside a man's head.

It seemed a perfectly sensible plan to me at the time.

Come to think of it, it still does. I mean, I wasn't setting out to make myself a hero to anybody. I was just mad as hell and wanted to get something back at Cap and any of the rest of them that got in my way. Afterward, well, I didn't exactly have a detailed plan worked out for that. I just figured to run like hell and get away into the night while the rest of the men were still confused and scared by being wakened by gunfire and the stink of fresh blood and powder smoke and scorched meat.

It might've worked out.

I'll never know.

49

THAT SOB CAP was the boss, that was obvious, and he had the power to make lies stick and then hang a man for them. But I'm telling you true, he was also one dumb son of a bitch. At least when it came to gambling he surely was.

Just standing outside that window and watching the way he played cards, I could see that he had no damn clue when it came to the odds of the game. Now I will grant that I couldn't see his cards nor anyone else's. But I could sure see his expression when he bet, so grim and determined as if he was bent and bound on winning each and every pot. He'd back a bad hand and overbet a good one, and I'm sure every other player at his table knew as easy as I did how good his cards were.

With an attitude like that, the man rarely won a hand and lost plenty of them. Fairly often, when he lost, he managed to lose big, and on those occasions when he won, he managed to win small.

The fellow was just a piss-poor cardplayer.

And those other boys in there weren't even cheating him. I can spot most of the tricks the professional card cheats pull. The card switches and cold-decking and bottom deals and shiny look-sees and all that. Lord knows I've kept company with enough cheats, frauds, and charlatans to know most of their ways, and these hay rakers and horse handlers wouldn't be in a class with the professionals. I was pretty sure there was no cheating going on at that table. Hell, they didn't need to cheat in order to beat the one they called Cap. He as good as emptied his pockets for them and asked them to take his money off him.

Which they did. A lot of it.

I could see plain as plain could be, and while they started out with mostly silver on the table, that changed fairly soon. The more Cap lost, the more he wanted to win back, and soon there was more gleam of yellow gold atop that table than there was the duller shine of silver.

I'd guess Cap must've lost over fifty dollars in the hour and a half, two hours I stood outside that window, watching him play and waiting for him to quit the game and go to bed so's I could shoot him.

That was more than a month's pay for most working hands, but Cap just kept digging deep and shoveling the money out for the others to take off him.

It was getting late by then and the rest of the crowd had pretty thoroughly dispersed, the men saying their good nights and wandering off to the bunkhouse or wherever, until finally there was only the five men playing at Cap's table left.

Not that I blamed those boys for staying up late. After all, they had a sheep in front of them just begging to be sheared, so what else could they do? Like any sensible sorts, if he insisted on giving money away, they were gonna sit there and take it from him.

Eventually, though, even the best of things has to end. I don't know if Cap ran out of money or it finally got through to him that he wasn't gonna win anything this night, but eventually, even this last table of players shuffled the pack a final time and snapped some gum-rubber bands around it. They yawned and stretched and stomped their feet to get the blood moving again when they stood, and one of them went around the room blowing out the lamps.

It was time for me to move, both because I didn't want to be seen peeping into windows and because I wanted to be around to see where Cap went from here.

I patted the hard lump in my back pocket where the Smith was and hurried around to the end of the building to stand behind a woodpile and watch.

I heard the door close and then a murmur of voices. Dark as it was, I could spot Cap because of the shape of his hat.

The other four walked off in the direction of the bunkhouse, but Cap, damn him, had a horse tied out front. He took a tug on his cinch and dropped his stirrup down and swung onto the saddle.

Apparently, the SOB didn't live here. Or anyway wasn't fixing to go to bed here tonight.

I thought about waiting outside the bunkhouse to see if he finally came back, but decided against that. There wasn't so much night left that it was reasonable to think he was going somewhere else and then would return here to sleep. More likely, I figured, as the boss he had another place.

And if he had another place to live, I wanted to find out where that was so I could complete my plan and put that bullet into his ear.

Better, I decided, to follow him.

It was dark enough that I could probably do that without being seen.

If somehow he managed to spot me, well, he was only one man, not seven now, and this time I'd have a gun to fight back with, never mind that it wasn't much of a gun.

I may be a lot of things, but I hope coward isn't one of them and I don't intend for it ever to be. Especially when I'm mad; and while my fuse may burn slow, it isn't easily extinguished. I *was* gonna get my own back, and I figured to start with this arrogant, stupid bastard who was sitting ahorseback so close in front of me right now.

Cap turned his horse around, wrapped his reins around the saddle horn, and lightly nudged the animal into a walk.

Perfect, I thought. He intended to sleep while the horse carried him home. And while I traipsed along behind.

The horse set off at a slow walk down the road, and so, by damn, did I.

50

NOW, WHO WOULD'VE thought it? Those people at the mine worked through the night. If anybody ever mentioned that to me, I'd sure gone and forgot it, but these guys were working several different shifts.

Which only made sense, I suppose. You get away down underground and you wouldn't be able to tell night from day anyhow. This, by the way, is information I take on faith and logic; no way I'm ever gonna find out for myself by going down there.

Anyway, one minute I was walking along behind that horse with its sleeping rider, myself being about as close to asleep as a body can manage while still being upright and moving, and the next thing I know there are voices and lights and movement up ahead and I have to stop in my tracks lest I walk right into somebody and give myself away.

The sound and the activity woke Cap up. I could see well enough to notice when he sat up out of the slumped-over slouch he'd been in while sleeping and took up his reins.

Somebody off to the left spoke to him—good thing too, for I hadn't spotted the man standing there—and Cap howdied him back.

Dang people were wandering around thick as ticks in a deer's ear. Or so it seemed. I had to lay back and watch from further and further away as Cap rode on, angling off the wagon road and toward his right.

I grunted and hunkered down beside the road to look and think for a spell. I would've left the road and followed on behind, but there was a building in that direction with lights showing behind the window shades, and I didn't want to take a chance on someone stepping outside and spotting me. Not until I'd worked out how I wanted to handle this.

It was a fairly noisy place despite the predawn hour. I could hear the dull thump of a stamp mill and voices and a distant recurring sound that I couldn't for a while identify. After hearing it repeated three or four times, I decided it was the sound of coal rattling down a chute up on the top of the cliff face. Apparently they freighted the coal over from wherever they dug it and then unloaded into a chute to carry it down to the levels where it was needed below. Made sense. But the noise sure spooked me until I figured out what it likely was.

As for Cap, the best I could do for the moment was to keep an eye on which direction he took and try to work out from that where to look for him.

I'd about half expected there to be a fence to worry about, but there wasn't, and once I realized that, I just swung wide around that building the man had rode past and hurried to try and catch up to him.

I didn't. And then I did. Caught up with him almost too well, in fact.

I was sidling past a set of corrals filled with mules and heavy horses and came up to what I thought was just a loafing shed where the livestock could get out from under the weather. Except it turned out the thing I'd mistaken for a shed was a long, low barn.

Cap opened a door I hadn't so much as seen and stepped out of it so close I like to ran into him.

"Excuse me, bub." Cap sidestepped to keep from walking smack into me and went on without bothering to look and see who I was. Which under the circumstances was just as well.

Me, I should've taken my chance and shot him there and then, I suppose, but the truth is that I was so startled that I never even thought of digging into that back pocket for my gun, nor it never occurred to me either that I could jump him. Take him by the throat and spit in his face or something. The son of a bitch. He'd hanged me. The bastard had gone and hanged me and here he was walking free while I was skulking around in the shadows.

Of course, by the time I thought all this and had a chance to get my blood to a boil, Cap was a dozen paces away and still walking.

I tugged my cap tighter onto a scalp that had begun to prickle some and set out again behind him.

✦ 51 ✦

SON OF A gun walked into what sure as shooting looked like a jail. Now, what a jail would be doing on the property of a private mining company I wouldn't have any idea. But this place damn sure looked to be enough like one as to make me plenty nervous.

I mean, there were bars on the windows and rocking chairs on the porch out front and everything, just like a real jail. Except if that SOB Cap was a proper law officer, they wouldn't have hanged me back on that mountain. And anyway the jail, if there was gonna be one, should be back in town, not out here.

It confused me. Cap, of course, acted like he was right at home. Which I expect he was, for apparently this was the place where he lived and never mind what it looked like.

He went inside without knocking, and before I could get a foot onto the porch, I heard the sound of a heavy bolt sliding home to securely lock the world out and me along with the rest of it.

Truth is that's probably just as well because if I'd gone up onto that porch, I'd've been sure to make some noise walking on the planks and then Cap would've come out and then we'd 've had to go to yanking triggers and sweating bullets, and who knows how I would've come out with nothing but that unfamiliar and undersized little .32 to shoot the man with. So I expect that all in all it's as well that he locked that door when he did.

Still, I didn't want to be this close and miss my chance at the peckerwood, so I slipped around to the back of the building—it wasn't much bigger than a family cabin, jail-like windows or no—to take a peek inside.

I could see in just fine, in the first place because it was all just one room with a pair of patent welded steel cells at the back, and in the second because Mr. Cap obliged my snooping by striking a lucifer match and lighting a table lamp on the side of a big desk. That helped guide me to a good spot for spying because of the sudden spill of light visible at a place where one of those roll-down blinds wasn't hanging quite tight against the window frame.

Cap replaced the globe over the lamp and shook the match out then tossed it into a cuspidor next to the desk. He walked over to the front door and tugged on it a couple times to make sure the bolt was holding and drew the blind down over the small window in the door too.

Whatever he was up to here he didn't want anybody else walking in on him while he was doing it. And that was even though as far as he knew, anyone else in the vicinity would have every right to be there.

Odd of him, I thought.

I kept on watching with plenty of interest while he knelt down beside the desk, moved the cuspidor aside and a rug, then lifted away a cunning little trapdoor sort of arrange-ment set into the floor.

Seemed he had something hidden, then. My interest was already high? It got higher still.

I saw him fiddling with something inside that hole in the floor that was down below my line of sight, then he lifted a metal door up and leaned it against the floorboards. From the way he moved it, I thought the door was on hinges but couldn't have sworn to that.

Cap looked over his shoulder like he halfway expected there was somebody watching him. Which of course there was, although he didn't know it. He looked back toward the cells and over to the tight-bolted front door.

Then he bent down and lifted out a canvas bank bag, one of those heavy bags with leather-and-steel collar-and-hasp arrangements that you can lock and that generally are used for carrying money or other mighty valuable small items. There was something printed on the canvas, but I couldn't make out the words from the window where I was doing my peeping.

The bag wasn't locked. He unfastened the hasp and opened it and reached down inside. Brought out a handful of little bitty objects and dropped them into his pants pocket. The same pocket I'd seen him taking money out of back at that card game where he was losing so heavy.

Now, it seemed, my boy Cap was putting money back *into* his pocket.

Taking it out of a bank bag and putting it into his own pocket.

Now, I'd guess there must be a thousand and one reasons why a man would go and do something like that.

I'll go that one step more and say there's probably a thousand and one *legal* reasons why a man would be doing such a thing.

In the middle of the night.

Behind a locked door.

Where he didn't want anyone to walk in nor to see.

Yeah. Right. A thousand and one good reasons.

But d'you know what? I bet I could come up with *ten* thousand and one *bad* reasons why a fella would be doing it too.

And while I was standing there looking in at Cap and his private money hole, a good half of those possible bad reasons were taking a swift canter through my thoughts.

My oh my, I thought to myself. Just what was it that we had here now? What, I do say what?

Cap took out whatever he'd wanted from the bag, closed the bag and put it back into the hole, dropped the metal door, and replaced the rug and cuspidor.

To look in there now you wouldn't know there was such a hidey-hole.

Cap stood and stretched, yawning, then went over and unbolted the door. He turned the lamp wick low but left it burning. I guessed he wasn't having to buy his own lamp oil.

He removed his gun belt and laid it onto the desk, stretched some more, and went back inside one of the cells, where he shook out a blanket, plumped up a flimsy little excuse for a pillow, and lay down to get some sleep while there was still a little nighttime remaining.

This was my chance, I thought. His gun was on the desk a good eight or ten feet away from where he was sleeping, and the door to the place was unlocked now.

All I had to do was give him a few minutes to drop off to sleep, then I could amble inside and plant a .32 slug behind his ear at my leisure. Simple as that.

I turned away from my place at the window and slid down onto the ground, sitting there with my feet—mighty painful feet they were by now too after walking so far— sticking straight out and my back against the wall of the mining-company jail or whatever this place was.

Ten minutes, I figured. Then I could just go inside and kill the son of a bitch.

✦ 52 ✦

I FELT A thump on the bottom of my shoe and woke up to bright sunshine and the sight of a man with a shotgun in his hands and a ferocious scowl on his face standing over top of me.

For one awful instant I thought he was one of those possemen come to take another crack at hanging me. My stomach flopped upside down and a frog jumped up into my throat and I thought I was gonna puke.

"I don't know what work detail you're ducking out on, buddy," he said, "and don't bother making up any lies. I don't wanta hear them, all right?"

This man was not one of the seven posse members, I realized. I'd never seen him before. Thank goodness. And he didn't sound half as growly as he looked.

"Whoever your boss is can worry about that. Right now I have something I need you to do. All right?"

I took another look at that shotgun. The guy was holding it, true, but he wasn't threatening me with it. He just happened to be holding it. "Sure," I told him. "Sure thing."

I got to my feet and followed him around to the front of the building where Cap had gone to sleep. And where I had too, dammit. I'd only intended to wait a few lousy minutes. Instead I'd dropped off into a deep sleep. Must've been more worn-out than I'd realized, what with all the walking and the late hour and just recovering from my injuries and everything. Now it was—I looked up into an almost cloudless sky—close on toward noon.

"Give me a hand with this, buddy," the guy said. In a friendly, offhand tone he added, "Some guy in town was gonna throw it away. Can you believe it? A fine sofa like this?"

The object in question was a ratty and tattered old piece of crap that once was a pretty nice couch with soft pillows and ribbed velveteen—I think that's what you would call it—upholstery. Blue. But that had been a long time ago. Now it looked like it'd spent the last couple years being used as a hotel for mice and roaches. I'd say it shouldn't have been thrown away. It should've been burned. As a public service.

Still, this guy with the shotgun seemed to think it was pretty wonderful. He'd managed to wrestle it into the back of a light wagon that was also loaded with sacks of flour and potatoes and cases of canned goods. The ratty old sofa was perched on top of his load.

He laid his shotgun onto the seat of the rig and came around back to drop the tailgate and motion for me to take an end of the sofa, which I did. "Where are we taking it?"

He inclined his head in the direction of the jaillike building, which in daylight and from this angle I could now see had a sign on the front that said SECURITY.

I dragged the sofa backward until he could grab the other end and finish lifting it off the wagon, then the two of us carried it onto the security-office porch and on through the door, me duckwalking backward while he took the easy end.

I went tight over the shoulders as I was backing indoors, wondering if Cap would recognize me despite my farmer clothes and what was now a full and fairly bushy beard.

As it turned out, Cap wasn't there. He'd gone to sleep in the right-hand cell, as I'd clearly seen through that side window, but at some point while I was outside sleeping, he woke up and took off.

I was just dumb lucky, I suppose, that he didn't spot me corked off there beside his security building.

"Over there, I think," the guy said, pointing with his chin.

He swung his end around and we sidestepped over to the wall where he wanted the couch placed. "There," he said with evident satisfaction once the thing was set down and he'd made some adjustments by nudging it with his hip and tugging on a filthy arm. "That is gonna be mighty comfortable when we have to spend nights in here."

I gathered that he meant they would be able to stretch out on it to nap. Not me, thank you. Sofa cushions might be softer to sleep on than a jail-cell bunk, but I wouldn't want me or any kin of mine to touch a cast-off mess like this couch was. No sirree. Still, it was his butt to risk, and if he wanted a fresh supply of lice he was surely welcome to them.

He grinned and sat down on one end of the thing and bounced and wiggled just a little.

I looked around, confirming the impressions of the place that I'd gotten earlier. I was careful to avoid staring at that rug where I knew Cap hid his money bag. Or somebody's money bag. I wasn't altogether convinced that it was Cap's.

"Whose office is this?" I asked, acting ignorant and friendly.

The security guy gave me a slightly odd look, then said, "Captain Meade, of course. You met him when you signed on."

"No, I don't think that was the name of the man I talked to," I told him.

"Must've been. Cap has to approve all the workers."

I shrugged. "Reckon I just forgot."

"Yeah, I know. There's a lot going on and everything's new. Guy can't be expected to remember everything, can he?"

I bobbed my head in perfect agreement.

"I'm Billy Coates," he volunteered, and offered his hand for a shake.

"Wes Johnson," I said, as that name was fresh in my mind lately. I hadn't any sooner than got the words past my teeth than I regretted saying them. I should've made up a new name just to make sure nothing I said or did here came back on Mrs. Kaufman and Evie.

Too late to think about that once the damage was done, though.

And I didn't really expect it to be anything I'd have to worry about.

I thought that by the end of the day I'd've had a chance to settle my score with that son of a bitch Cap Meade and be on my way to see some city lights.

"Thanks for helping me with this," Coates said.

"Sure," I told him. "Glad to."

"I have to get that stuff over to the cookhouse."

"Yeah, and I suppose I'd better get back to work too," I said. Which was the truth of a sort, although not exactly in the way of what Billy Coates might be thinking. "D'you mind if I sit here for a couple minutes first? This sofa of yours looks mighty soft."

"I expect that'd be all right, Wes. Help yourself."

I did. I cringed some at the thought of sitting on that dirty thing—Lord only knew what kind of vermin were scurrying around inside those pillows—but I managed to not show it.

And the couch was soft. Filthy and ugly but soft.

"I'll be back soon as this wagon is unloaded," Coates said.

"Oh, I won't be here that long, I'm sure." I meant that too. Something had occurred to me once I was inside and I saw that Cap Meade was not. And it was an even better idea than putting a bullet into that man's ear.

Coates gave me a wave good-bye and went outside. Nice fella, actually.

I jumped up and hurried over to peep out a window. Coates climbed onto the driving box and shoved his shotgun under the seat, then took up the lines and got the team to pulling. The wagon rattled off into the middle of the complex of buildings that made up the mine.

Coates hadn't gone ten yards before I was on the floor kneeling over that hidey-hole where Cap Meade kept his money bag.

✦ 53 ✦

SON OF A *bitch*!

It wasn't just a steel box he'd sunk into the ground here, it was a small but stoutly made floor safe complete with a combination lock on it.

Made sense. That's why he'd needed light last night in order to get into it and explained what he'd been doing when he was fiddling with it down inside where I hadn't been able to see.

Meade had himself a just fine hidey-hole here.

My thought had been that if Meade kept a whole bunch of money in his floor box, I could kinda appropriate it as compensation for the five thousand him and his pals had stolen off of me.

As to where he might've gotten it—well, I had a few suspicions about that too, damn him. And none of the possibilities that came to mind were charitable toward Mr. Meade.

Anyway, where it came from and whoever it properly belonged to, I'd figured that once I had the money in hand, then I could give thought to whether I wanted to press this thing by trying to shoot Meade and maybe some of those other boys . . . or just slide quietly out of this valley and let them all go to hell without my connivance.

Unfortunately, dammit, it wasn't going to be that easy.

I put the rug back down and was kneeling there trying to remember just exactly how that cuspidor had been placed—I didn't want to change any least thing that would give away the fact that somebody knew his secret—when I heard footsteps strike the boards on the porch outside.

I jumped up and gave the room a wild-eyed look around. But there wasn't any place to run to.

The door swung open and I found myself nose to nose with Cap Meade.

✢ 54 ✢

I COULDN'T TELL if he recognized me or not. Probably not. My appearance was different now and anyway no one expects to find himself looking at a walking, talking dead man. So I really doubt that Meade knew me for the fellow he'd hanged up on that mountain.

But then he really didn't need to think back that far in order to know that something was wrong here. The rug was in place where it was supposed to be, but that dang cuspidor had been moved off it and I hadn't yet got it back where it belonged.

One glance from me to the cuspidor and back and Cap Meade knew that this deal was not to his liking.

He went for his gun.

I went for the door.

As it happened, Meade was standing squarely between me and the door and one of us or the other was gonna have to give.

Meade just about had time to grab his pistol and start lifting it free of leather when I lowered my shoulder and gave my best effort at disconnecting his head from the rest of him.

I bowled into him like he was a duckpin and I was the ball. I've no idea what it felt like to him, but when I hit him, the impact was hard enough to put a hurting into me.

Not that it slowed me down any. Not hardly. I ran smack through him, knocking him aside and clearing the way for me to get out that door.

The force of it jarred the pistol out of his hand and sent it spinning across the room. I don't know if he'd had time enough to cock it already—he'd have to've been plenty fast if so—but for whatever reason, the gun went off when it hit the floor.

You think spurs will get a horse to moving or a goad take an ox down the road? You don't know what a truly sincere motivation for motion can be until you've heard a gunshot at your back.

And by then my back was all that was visible from inside that security office, let me tell you. I'd've caught and passed a jackrabbit right then and you give the rabbit a head start. Believe it.

Out onto that porch and away.

But on foot. And in broad daylight. And with Meade and his gun still back there in the office. It wasn't going to take him very long to get that pistol back into his hands, and I knew it.

I saw a wagon hauling a load of hay in from the direction of that ranch where I'd spotted Meade the night before. Saw some fellows walking slow and tired from the mine toward what I took to be a barracks or boardinghouse sort of affair. Saw a handsomely dressed man in a suit coat and those tall, lace-up boots that engineers favor riding out onto the road to town. Saw an awful lot of very empty space between me and the creek, where the nearest brush could be found for hiding-in purposes.

It didn't take me much time to sort out which of those interested me. Not even a little bit.

I ran straight at that engineer. He saw me coming. Might've seen Meade storming along behind me, I wouldn't know. For whatever reason, he reined his little chestnut saddler to a halt and kinda sat there staring and blinking in confusion about it all. Bless him. I'm mighty grateful that he wasn't quicker on the uptake, believe me.

I didn't bother trying to explain the situation or apologize. Just threw myself at the guy. Grabbed him and wrestled him down off his horse into the dirt and, before the startled animal could bolt away from me, took a death grip on the saddle horn.

The horse, being somewhat more sensible than its rider when it came to knowing what to do when spooked, lifted into a hard run straight from the standing start.

Which was just what I would've had in mind anyway.

That first jump like to snatched my arm clean out of its socket, but I wasn't about to let a little inconvenience like that get in the way of things. I let it carry me along, clinging to that saddle horn tight as any tick could've done. Along about the second or third stride I managed to get my other hand onto the horn and take my weight onto my arms, swung my legs ahead, and then kicked down hard onto the ground that was rushing by. Between the force of my own jump and the forward motion of the horse, I was able to bounce high enough to get a leg over the horse's rump.

That was all I needed. Give me a leg and one good handhold and there hasn't been a horse foaled yet that can get me off again. Not that day there wasn't, anyway.

I dragged myself the rest of the way onto the saddle and reached for the reins. I wasn't quite quick enough. The reins were flying free, and the horse stepped on one. His head snatched hard around and I thought for half a second he was gonna go down and take me with him, but the rein snapped in two, and the horse regained his balance and so did I.

Back behind me I heard a gunshot and then another. I didn't look to see was it Meade doing the shooting or someone else. What I was pretty sure about was that, busted rein or not, there wasn't any hay wagon gonna catch up with me. Not while I was mounted and moving.

Half a minute more and I was beyond the range of even a rifle. I was able to sit up in the saddle then and give some thought to getting a bit of control over that scared horse's mad tear across the valley floor.

✦ 55 ✦

I LEFT THE horse tied by its one good rein, standing not too, too deep inside a willow thicket. After all, I wanted someone to find it, just not too soon. First I needed time to slide down along the creek to the anonymity of town.

Figured I'd need time and place as well to hide out for a spell while I thought about what I should—or could—do next.

And that meant that I'd be going back to the Kaufman farm for at least a few days. This time, though, I wouldn't be going empty-handed.

I finally had both opportunity and daylight in which to investigate the coins I'd stolen off that unfortunate drunk. I pulled the dinner rolls out of my left-hand pocket only to find they been mashed and mangled beyond usefulness, so I left the crumbs for the birds to enjoy and munched on a raw potato while I walked along the creek bank and counted my ill-gotten money.

The fellow I'd robbed must've been paid recently, because there was some yellow mixed in with the silver coins. Two of what had felt like dimes turned out to be ten dollar pieces. In all, the change amounted to twenty eight dollars and twenty cents. Hell, I was halfway toward being rich.

I stayed inside the creekside brush until I was close to

town, then went out onto the public road and walked in plain sight the rest of the way, past the two churches that stood at the west end of town and on into the business district.

It was late afternoon by then but the stores were still open. And I did have some shopping to do before I hiked out east to the Kaufmans' place.

The first thing I needed was a gun. A proper one, not some poopy little .32 Smith & Wesson. I could have saved some money by trading the Smith in on something better, but I knew better than that. Hard money has no identifying features but guns sure do, and I didn't want anyone spotting that Smith as having been stolen and following it back to me. So I left the Smith secure in my pocket and laid out seven of my ill-gotten dollars for a much worn but still reasonably tight Remington revolver in .44–40 caliber.

"You guarantee it to shoot?" I asked the man behind the store counter.

He nodded. "I do. Guarantee it to shoot. Don't guarantee you can hit anything with it, though."

"That's fair enough," I said. And so it was. The truth is that there's not too awful many men who can hit a bull in the butt with a handgun even if they're standing close enough to use the gun as a club instead. "Just so it will fire."

"It will fire," the fellow assured me. "Want to walk out back to the creek and see for yourself?"

"Good idea."

"Pay for the ca'tridges and help yourself."

I took him up on it. There wasn't much daylight left by then, but the visibility was good enough that I found out the Remington shot a little high but otherwise was all right.

"I'll take it," I told the man when I went back inside. "And two boxes of .44s to go with it. And . . . can you deliver an order for me? I want to buy a bunch of stuff, but I don't have a wagon or a wheelbarrow to carry it all."

"Mister, if you're buying that much, I'll get it to wherever you're staying. Won't be until tomorrow, but I'll get it there."

"Fair enough," I said again. I laid the rest of my money—well, it *was* mine now—on the counter and said, "Tell me when I run out of buying power, will you? Now first off, I need some fine ground wheat flour. And a little coffee, I think. And some of those dried beans there. And canned meats. And . . ."

Between him and me we came up with a list that included more stuff than I could've managed if I'd had Mrs. Kaufman's wheelbarrow with me. I took a small bag of flour, some ready-ground coffee, a chunk of bacon, and a pound of dried butter beans to carry with me, and he promised to have the rest of my order delivered no later than noon the next day.

I packed what I intended to carry along with me into a burlap sack that he tossed in free for nothing—that included the Remington and cartridges—and slung the bag over my shoulder for the long walk back to the Kaufman farm.

It was dark by the time I set off down the road again. I was tired and I suppose I could've slept alongside the creek for the night, but the truth is that I was anxious to put some real food, meat and all, into Mrs. Kaufman's pot.

So I walked on, my feet aching by now but otherwise feeling pretty good about things.

Some ideas were already beginning to germinate about how I should handle Cap Meade and his friends. A few days of laying low and eating high and I thought I could have that worked out.

I was dead wrong about that. But I thought it at the time.

✦ 56 ✦

M Y BACK ACHED, my feet still hurt, and my hands stung like fire. Funny thing was that I was feeling actually pretty chipper. I'd been able to keep up with Mrs. Kaufman chopping weeds in the cornrows this morning, and I felt kinda proud of that. Certainly it was a first-time accomplishment.

Next thing you knew, I might could learn to milk a dang cow too. Why, I was beginning to think I was getting a handle on this farmer stuff after all.

"More bacon gravy, Mr. Johnson?"

"I believe I will, ma'am, thank you." I ladled a big, thick, stand-up-by-itself dollop of the good gravy onto a lighter-than-feathers wheat-flour biscuit and passed the gravy boat to Evie, who seemed to be enjoying this food I'd brought every bit as much as I did. To the point that I was hanging back and going light on the bacon so she could fill up on it.

There would be more coming along shortly. I hadn't been able to carry all that much with me last night.

As it was, Mrs. Kaufman had a pot of the dried beans set aside to soak in time for supper. And when the wagon got here with the rest of the stuff, there would be some dried apples too. If I played my cards right and begged real hard, maybe I could talk her into making a pie for us too. It's a fact that I do enjoy apple pie and a big glass of milk to go with it. I was betting Evie would like that too, which would be my ace in the hole when I got around to asking her mama for the favor.

"Somebody's coming," Evie said.

I cocked my head to the side and listened. The kid was right. I could hear it too now she'd mentioned it.

"That should be the man with the rest of the groceries," I said.

"You didn't have to do this, you know," Mrs. Kaufman said.

I just shrugged. Last night I'd told her I won some money gambling when I was in town. She'd accepted the lie without asking where I'd come up with the wherewithal to start playing. Probably hadn't thought about that, which was just fine with me.

For some reason it kinda bothered me to be telling false-hoods to this woman. And that, I'm afraid, isn't much like me. Not usually.

Anyway, I could hear the approach of horses clear now. I stood up from the table and folded my napkin and laid it beside my plate.

"I'd best help unload," I said. "Evie, don't you go to poaching my biscuits and gravy there. I got my portion counted, and I'll be watching close when I come back."

She giggled and made like she was gonna stab her fork onto my plate. I winked at her and went outside.

That was damn near the last thing I ever did in this world.

✢ 57 ✢

IT WASN'T SOME friendly merchant I found out there but Captain Meade and a damn posse.

Some of them were even the same sons of bitches who'd robbed and hanged me.

They were coming for me again, and I went cold as death when I saw them.

I liked to froze up solid at that first glance. My belly felt hollow and empty despite the meal I'd just packed away, and the crazy thought came into my head that if I moved they'd kill me, but if I stood stone still maybe they'd miss seeing me and ride on by.

That was stupid, of course, and it didn't last long.

Two or three heartbeats—and believe me, those were coming unnatural quick of a sudden—and that initial spell of immobilizing fear vanished.

Before they could snatch their guns out, I jumped backward into Mrs. Kaufman's place and slammed the door shut. There was a heavy wood bar for the door. I hadn't ever seen it used before, but it was there and I used it now. Dropped it into place to secure the door and dashed across the room to the burlap sack where I'd left my gun and cartridges so Mrs. Kaufman and Evie wouldn't see and go to wondering.

With time to think about the situation and work it all out, I suppose the right and decent thing for me to do would've been to keep my fight outside.

But dammit, I didn't have a gun with me except for the wee .32 that was still in my hind pocket, and there were five of those sons of bitches riding down on me.

I consider myself a fairly decent shot with a belly gun, but I wouldn't claim that I could take out five mounted men with the five little bitty slugs out of that Smith & Wesson.

I just naturally reacted and got the hell under cover without taking time to think about it.

That was something of a mistake, I suppose, and I plead guilty to it. But I did it, and once done, there wasn't any way to change it.

And once those five riders were dismounted and had their guns out and looking for a target, there just wasn't any way I was gonna abandon the protection of four walls and go charging at them in the open. Call me a coward if you like, but that woulda been more than a little bit stupid.

So I barred the door and turned to tell Mrs. Kaufman and Evie to get down.

I didn't have time to get the warning out of my mouth before Meade and his posse opened fire.

The gunshots made a dull, barking sound outside, and there was a flurry of accompanying thumps as bullets slammed into the door and the walls and a couple of them shattered glass in the windows.

Whoever was shooting at the windows was one dumb so-and-so, because the windows were small and set high under the eaves of the roof so they could be left open to allow for the movement of air even in bad weather. Anybody standing outside and shooting through those couldn't expect to hit anything inside except the ceiling or maybe the sleeping loft. Dumb.

"Mr. Johnson!" There was concern in Mrs. Kaufman's

voice but no panic. This was a woman who had some sand in her.

"I'm sorry, ma'am. Those men are after me."

"Do they have reason, Mr. Johnson?"

I grinned at her. "Yes, ma'am, they surely do. They robbed me and left me for dead a while back. When I came here I was following them." My grin got wider. "Looks like I found them, all right."

"Yes, I would say that you most certainly did."

"Sorry 'bout this, ma'am. I surely never meant to lead them here."

"I am sure you did not," she said. Which was nice of her, because out in the yard Meade and his boys were still firing off shots that thumped and thudded into the door and the walls.

I waited for a lull in the shooting, then stood underneath one of the windows and shouted, "Yo, out there. Meade! There's a woman and little girl in here. You don't have any quarrel with them. Let them go."

"No, you come out. We'll arrest you and take you into town. You'll stand a fair trial, mister. Surrender yourself and no one will be harmed."

"Arrest me for what?" I asked. "I've done nothing to be arrested for."

"You're charged with assault on a peace officer and stealing a horse," Meade shouted back. "Better a few months behind bars than to be shot trying to resist a lawful arrest."

"Kinda like the last time you arrested me?" I asked.

"I never saw you before yesterday," he said.

I'd wondered about that. Now I knew. He hadn't recognized me. But he knew that I was aware of that hidey-hole of his, and he wouldn't want me left alive to be able to tell anybody about it.

I thought I knew how they'd got onto me, damn them. I'd used my Wes Johnson handle with I talked to Coates out there at the mine yesterday. And between that and my description, I guess it hadn't been that difficult for them to track me to the store in town and find out where I'd gone to ground.

I felt like the worst kind of fool to've brought this trouble onto Mrs. Kaufman and the kid. I should've thought. But I hadn't, and now it was too late to go back and change anything.

"You'll promise me a fair trial?" I shouted through the window.

"You have my word on it," Meade shouted back.

"Same sort of fair trial you gave me last time? When you robbed me of five thousand dollars and hanged me on that mountain? That kind of fair trial, you son of a bitch?"

"You can't—" Meade blurted that out, then stopped. I kinda wished I could've seen his face right then. Bet he was shocked to hear that his hanging hadn't taken.

And then I did what has to be the stupidest thing I've ever done in my entire life. I shouted at him, "I figured out why you wanted somebody to pin that payroll robbery on, Meade. You stole it yourself, damn you, and I can prove it."

Stupid? I reckon and then some.

Because once Mrs. Kaufman and Evie heard those words out of the mouth that sat at the front of my empty head, Meade would want them dead too so they couldn't repeat my accusation.

I realized that about two seconds after it was too damn late.

Meade's answer was another gunshot, and his men quickly joined in with a fresh outburst of firing.

I gave Mrs. Kaufman a look of apology and hoped that she didn't realize what I'd just gone and done to her and to her little girl.

✠ 58 ✠

I'D BEEN IN worse places than this and survived to gloat about it after. I kept telling myself that. And, hey, this time that old phrase was even true. That little incident with the hanging came to mind, for instance. And there'd been other times that . . . well, never mind about them.

Besides, I was too busy to be wasting any time with idle thinking.

I grabbed Mrs. Kaufman's bed, the one where she'd parked me while I recuperated from my hurts, and dragged it underneath the window on the right side of the house. Shoved a chair under the left side window. Put a storage trunk under one of the two windows in the front wall.

All the while I was doing that I was regretting that there wasn't any threat of Indian attack in this part of the country. If there still had been, maybe the late Mr. Kaufman would've built with defense of his house in mind and put some firing ports into the walls or like that. As it was, this house was going to be difficult to defend and in the long run impossible.

You see, there was no window on the back side of the house, and that was going to be the problem.

Sooner or later Meade would get around to setting the

house on fire, and there just wouldn't be any way I could keep the men away from that wall.

The fire wouldn't come right away, though. I was pretty sure I could count on that.

The men who were out there with Meade . . . I was banking on the idea that they weren't completely aware of why it was so important to Cap Meade now that me and Mrs. Kaufman and even little Evie die inside this house. And especially with none of us having a chance to talk to anyone who had a clear conscience.

Meade wanted what I knew to die in here, but he needed the help of his posse in order to get that done. It would take him a while, I figured, before he could get them worked up to the point that they'd be willing to set a house afire while there were innocent females inside.

Wouldn't cause any of them any heartburn to shoot me down or burn me out, but Mrs. Kaufman and Evie were a different deal altogether.

And I sure wanted to keep them all reminded about it.

So I stood atop the linen chest or whatever that storage trunk was and hollered out, "Let the woman and little girl go. I'll fight you square but let them go."

I got a gunshot in return. Which was what I'd expected. Figured it was likely fired by Meade himself, and finding out where he was hiding was one of the things I wanted to know.

It would please hell out of me if I could put a bullet between that man's horns, and I would right thoroughly enjoy shooting at him once I knew where to shoot.

But I had no desire at all to shoot at any of those other fellows. The less I worried them or made them mad, the longer it would take them to be convinced that they should do Meade's murdering for him and start that fire.

So my reasons were twofold. Remind those possemen that Mrs. Kaufman and Evie were in here. And see if I couldn't spot where that SOB Meade was.

I peeped out the corner of the window, exposing myself

as little as I could manage, and spotted the powder smoke from that last gunshot. The guy—likely Meade—was standing inside the barn, just to my right side of the door.

Did a little thinking then. The walls of this house were stout and the door built up from hand-hewn timber. Unless somebody had a powerful rifle out there like a Sharps or a Martini, they weren't likely to get a bullet through the house door. Not unless they pecked away shot after shot for a good long while they wouldn't, for an ordinary revolver cartridge or saddle carbine load isn't all that strong. It would take something on the order of a buffalo rifle to bust through the wood in this door.

The barn wall, on the other hand, was made of much lighter stuff. There was a good chance that a pistol bullet would rip through it and still have force enough to do some damage on the other side.

I calculated where Meade's belly should be if he was still standing in that same spot, aimed nice and careful, and popped a round off.

Didn't know for sure if I hit anyone or who or how bad . . . but my shot sure did provoke a yelp from outta that barn. If I didn't manage to shoot the son of a bitch, I must've dusted him with splinters at the very least.

And under the circumstances, I was willing to settle for whatever I could get.

Naturally, everybody out there reacted. There was a roar of gunfire enough to make you think a horde of wild Indians, Mongol invaders, and government revenuers was all out there burning powder.

Bullets thumped and banged against the walls like hail on a roof, and inside half a minute there wasn't a single shard of glass left in any of Mrs. Kaufman's windows.

I was still standing on that trunk and felt a light touch on the side of my leg. I looked down and seen—saw—Mrs. Kaufman standing there.

"Ma'am, you and Evie oughta be on the floor somewhere. Over behind the iron stove maybe. That'd be the safest place."

"What is this all about, Mr. Johnson?"

I thought about that but only for a couple seconds. Hell, she had a right to know. If Meade was able to exercise control over his people out there, she might well die because of it, her and her little girl too. She really had a right.

So I emptied my gun through the window to keep them more or less honest, not aiming and deliberately shooting high so I wouldn't hit anybody that I didn't want to, then stepped down to the floor and while I reloaded began explaining the situation to Mrs. Kaufman.

I F IT WASN'T so damned serious, this business of being under siege could be really boring.

We'd all more or less settled down. Every once in a while one of the possemen would shoot a little to show us they were still out there. Every once in a while I'd go to one of the windows and shout something about them letting Mrs. Kaufman and the child go unharmed. My reminders weren't exactly subtle but then it was substance I was interested in here and not style.

The shadows that'd been pointed toward town when the posse showed up changed direction and started slanting off toward the desert end of the valley instead.

Even little Evie got over being so scared and began grumbling about being hungry, so Mrs. Kaufman cooked us all some lunch. No bacon, though. We'd finished all I carried out from town the evening before.

Naturally, once the stove was stoked up and drawing, Meade saw that and had one of his boys go around back to where I couldn't see and climb onto the roof. I could hear him up there and might've been able to shoot through the roof and hit him, but I didn't try. Still didn't want to make anybody out there except Meade mad at me.

The guy stopped up the chimney in the hope they could

smoke us out like bees in a hive, but I'd been expecting that and pulled the fire just as quick as I heard the sounds of him moving overhead. The worst it did was let a little wood smoke into the house, just enough to make our eyes sting and Evie coughed a bit, but all in all it wasn't serious. And there was enough heat in the stove for Mrs. Kaufman's biscuits to bake and her gravy to form. The gravy was a little lumpy, which wasn't at all like she usually did, but it tasted just fine anyway.

"Biscuits and gravy, boys," I yelled out a window. "Mrs. Kaufman sure does cook 'em fine."

Only one gun shot back at the sound. Meade again, I would've bet.

I wondered what those other boys were thinking.

"You said you expect them to burn us out?" Mrs. Kaufman asked.

"Yes, ma'am, I do."

"When do you think that would happen, Mr. Johnson?"

I polished off the last of my lunch and set the plate down. "Won't be until after dark, I'd think. It's . . . it's easier to get men to do ugly things, ma'am, when they have the dark to cover them while they're doing it. Meade will know that. I don't think he'll bring it up to them until then. And once he does"—I shrugged—"depends on how blindly those boys will follow him. No way to tell now what he'll tell them to get them worked up or how he'll handle it. Could be he'll get them drunk first. Could be he'll try and convince them with sweet talk. Maybe he'll get them with offers of a big reward in cash money. He'll know his men, and I expect he'll use whatever he can to get them to do his dirty work." I smiled at her. "But we don't have to worry about it much until past dark."

"Thank you, Mr. Johnson." She turned and began gathering our dirty dishes into a pail even though she didn't have enough clean water inside to wash them with. And it wouldn't be a real good idea for anybody to step out to the well right now.

"Mrs. Kaufman."

"Yes, Mr. Johnson?" She paused, facing away from me, not looking back over her shoulder.

"I just wanted to mention, ma'am, that you are an uncommonly handsome woman. Your husband was a might lucky man."

I have *no* idea where that came from. God knows I never consciously expected to say it. My only excuse is that we were fixing to die fairly soon and . . . well, I said it. That's all. I did.

She turned. I could see she was plenty surprised. Which was reasonable enough. So was I.

She didn't say anything, just stood there looking at me for a bit. Then she turned around again and went back to collecting dishes that might never get washed.

I felt some heat in my ears.

But I didn't regret what I'd said. Dammit, I did not. It was true, as I'd surely come to notice over these past weeks. Kaufman really had been one lucky man. Except for being dead now, that is.

I climbed up onto the chair at the side window and loosed off a cylinder full of .44s to let them know we weren't dead yet.

✛ 60 ✛

"OH, DAMN!" I blurted. Didn't even care that Evie could hear.

"What's wrong, Mr. Johnson?"

"Horses. I can hear horses coming. Meade must've sent for more men."

"What does that mean?"

"Could be he intends to get this over with now an' not wait for dark. Could be they're gonna storm the place."

"Can we do anything to stop them?"

"Not really. Look, I'll do what I can, but it won't really matter much. If there's enough of them coming and just one gun firing back . . . they can find something to use for a batter and knock the door down. It won't hold but awhile. I want—I'm sorry, ma'am; I can't tell you how sorry I am about this—but what I want you t' do now is to take Evie and hide her under the bed. You get under there with her. Put her up tight against the wall and then you lie down beside her. I'll pile up whatever I can find to hide you. You oughta be safe from bullets there when they get inside. And those men . . . they aren't all of them like Meade is. They won't find it easy to shoot down a lady and a child. So you lay real still and don't cause any commotion. They'll find you eventually, but you let it take as long as possible before you come out. Okay?"

Her eyes, more blue than gray right now I thought, were big and sorrowful. She looked at me without speaking for a time.

"Go on now, ma'am. I can hear wagon traces. They may've brought a ram with them. Take Evie and get under there like I told you."

She nodded and took the mute and terrified little girl's hand. The both of them crawled under the bed like I'd directed, and I got busy piling stuff in front of them, trying to fill in the space underneath the bed and on top of it with stuff thick and heavy enough to stop bullets.

I was still busy doing that when some damn fool knocked on the door.

That's right. Stepped up to the door and knocked on it like company asking to come in.

I quit looking for stuff to throw onto the bed and flipped open the loading gate of my revolver to make sure it was stuffed full and ready to go.

The guy outside knocked again, and I moved over to crouch behind the stove and get ready for them to come swarming inside.

✢ 61 ✢

"MRS. KAUFMAN? ARE you in there? Are you all right?" It was a new voice, not Meade.

"Mrs. Kaufman? This is Don Payne. Are you all right? What is going on here?"

I could hear Mrs. Kaufman trying to get out from behind all the junk I'd crammed in front of her. I left her to it and jumped up onto the trunk that was at the front window.

There was a whole heap of people outside. Not just Meade and his posse but the banker Payne, just like he'd said, and a bunch of folks, most of whom I'd never laid eyes on before. I did recognize the man from the store who was supposed to deliver supplies out here today—I'd forgotten about him, but then I do have the excuse of having been distracted by other matters of more immediate interest—and Paul Mackey from the saloon in town. And of course Payne, who was dressed like a banker ought to be.

The men were holding a wild assortment of shotguns, rifles, and pistols, and there was one fellow—turned out to be the neighbor from the next farm over—who had come with nothing but a pitchfork to fight with.

And these men had damn sure come ready to fight.

Payne had said the community knew and liked Mrs. Kaufman and Evie? I reckon they did at that. Soon as the storekeeper—Adderley, his name was—heard the gunfire at the Kaufman farm, he turned and raced back to town. With Payne leading them, they came larruping back with a posse to surround Captain Meade's posse and make sure no one was gonna bring harm to that woman nor to her little girl.

"He did *what*?" Payne demanded when I started in to explaining what was what here.

"I told you. He hanged me, damn him."

"You can't be him," Meade blurted. He tried to lunge for me, but Mackey and the neighbor man Charles Brady had a good grip on him and wouldn't turn him loose.

"But I am, you son of a bitch." I explained how I'd come to be here, alive, instead of out on that mountain providing feed for the pine jays and magpies.

"You say they took five thousand dollars from you?"

"Yes, sir. Those men in the posse, I'd guess they didn't honestly know any different. They really thought it was me that robbed your payroll money. But it wasn't. It was Meade there. He was in charge of it, and he stole it himself. I can show you where he keeps it. And I can tell you what sort of container it was in too." I described the bank bag that I'd seen when I spied on Meade through that window.

"You would know that if you really were the one who stole the money," Payne observed.

"Yes sir, I would. But if I'd stole it I sure wouldn't have left it—*and* the money in it—in a floor safe in Meade's own office, would I? And I couldn't have done that and still had another five thousand on me when they snuck up to my camp and robbed me.

"Meade caught me inside his office yesterday, and while he didn't know I was the same fella he thought he pinned the crime on and hanged already, he did know that I'd found out about that safe. That's why he wanted me dead now and that's why he was scared to leave Mrs. Kaufman and Evie alive too. He couldn't know how much I'd told them. He was gonna goad these men in his posse into killing all of us. Ask them. I bet they won't stand by him now they know the truth about him."

They didn't either. To a man the men who'd rode out here beside Captain Meade turned on him now they knew he was playing them for suckers and trying to make murderers of them to protect his own backside.

Once they knew, the townspeople who'd come out with Payne to help Mrs. Kaufman had to protect Captain Meade. From his own posse. They were that mad at him.

They told Payne in detail how Meade tried to prod them into burning the house with a woman and child inside.

That was all it took to seal Meade's fate. His only luck of the day was that Payne managed to keep them from hanging him.

Apart from that, well, he'd had better days. And I'd sure as hell had worse ones.

"We'll have to confirm what you've told us, Mr. Johnson," Payne said once Meade was trussed up and dumped into the back of John Adderley's wagon. "But I suspect your story will prove out. You do understand, of course, that the money taken from you was turned in as the recovered payroll and was distributed to the employees at the mine."

"Yes, sir, and I also realize that some of that payroll Meade stole has already been gambled away. But that bag looked fairly heavy when he took it out the other night. And I figure whatever is in there belongs t' me now, since my money covered the original loss."

Payne frowned. But then no banker ever likes to see a dollar leave his hands. He harrumphed and coughed a couple times and didn't exactly concur right out loud. But I had no doubt he'd see the light in my argument by and by. "We'll see," was all he said.

That was enough for me.

Hell, if nothing else, I was still alive when the two posses, Meade's and Payne's, started back to Willow Creek with Ed Meade tied like a shoat on its way to market. Or to slaughter, a thought which I rather preferred.

✢ 62 ✢

"YOU'RE BACK," MRS. Kaufman observed when I walked into the house a week and a half later. It wasn't exactly a comment that needed answering.

"Did you . . . is everything all right now?"

"He paid over the money, if that's what you mean." I grinned at her. "He didn't much like having to part with it. And he kept his dang bank bag. But he paid out what was there."

I was also, by damn, wearing my own good hat and my own good boots, and outside was standing my own horse with my saddle on it. The stuff had been gathered up from some real sheepish members of that hanging posse. Whoever had my Colt and gun belt hadn't owned up to it, but most everything else was recovered. I guess I was gonna pass on the idea of looking up those other six and punching them out. The hell with it.

"It wasn't everything they took, though, was it?" she said.

I shrugged. "It was more'n I really expected." More than three thousand, actually. Three thousand two hundred and forty-six, to be precise. That Meade sure could run money through his hands in a big hurry, damn him.

Not that I had any real right to complain. Hell, I'd stole

it myself off a freight agent down near Tombstone. The yarn I'd told those boys up on the mountain, that was just my regular way of doing. My whole life has been a lie, a cheat, or a steal one way or another.

Here, looking at Mrs. Kaufman, I could feel regrets of a sort I'd never felt before, and was having thoughts that I'd sure never thought before.

"I suppose you'll be going on your way now," she said. I strained to hear if I could detect either pleasure or unhappiness in her voice when she said it. But I couldn't.

I stood there looking out toward the barn where the Jerseys Lou Cow and Blue Cow and whatever the hell else they were named had started coming in for their evening milking. Thought about all the sweaty, miserable work it took to raise up a plot of corn or take a scythe and hand-mow a stand of grain.

Farming is a hard way of life.

So is living honest and raising a family and just being . . . ordinary. That wasn't something I'd given much thought to before now.

It was a lousy life and only a damn fool would put up with it.

I dug around in my beard. It'd begun to itch again. "I dunno," I said.

"You have your money back. There's nothing to hold you here now."

"No, I reckon there isn't."

"Do you want to wait until morning? We'll be having salt pork and a dried-apple pie for supper tonight."

"I like dried-apple pie."

"Yes," she said. "I know. You told me that once."

My right ear itched too. I scratched it. "I don't have a job."

"No, I suppose you don't."

"You could hire me on. You need help around the place. You and the kid could show me how to do all this stuff."

She kinda smiled. Then—I thought she sighed a little bit

first—she said, "I don't have any money to hire a man."

I grinned at her. "You would if I loaned you enough t' take on a hired man."

Those huge, pale eyes widened. "How much of a wage do you demand, sir?"

"Top wage," I said. "And plenty of milk. An' dried-apple pie every Sunday."

"Thinking of Sundays, Mr. Johnson, if I hire a man I'll expect him to attend services with us."

I like to balked on that one. I mean . . . hell. I didn't so much as know what the inside of one of them places looked like.

"That's firm, ma'am?"

She nodded.

I rubbed the side of my nose. "But there'd be the dried-apple pie after?"

She nodded again.

I felt aflutter inside my belly, as scared I think or more so than when those SOBs put the rope around my neck.

"You got yourself a hired man, ma'am." Lordy, but I felt funny saying that. Jumpy and nervous as I'd ever been in my life.

"Mr. Johnson . . . Wes . . ."

"Yes, ma'am?"

"I think you can start calling me Catherine."

I guess I was smiling then. And so was she.